Vital Signals

Vital Signals
Virtual Futures Near-Future Fictions

Edited by
Dan O'Hara, Tom Ward, Stephen Oram

NewCon Press
England

First edition, published in the UK January 2022
by NewCon Press
41 Wheatsheaf Road, Alconbury Weston, Cambs, PE28 4LF

NCP 271 (hardback)
NCP 272 (softback)

10 9 8 7 6 5 4 3 2 1

'Brain Gun' by Paul Green was originally published in the collection *The
Gestaltbunker* (Shearsman Books, 2012)
'An Excerpt from the Post-Truth and Irreconcilable Differences Commission'
by Brendan C. Byrne was originally published on www.imperica.com/ in April
2018.
'Biohacked & Begging' by Stephen Oram was originally published in the
collection *Biohacked & Begging* (SilverWood Books, 2019)
'Trial By Combat' by John Houlihan was originally published in the collection
The Constellation of Alarion and Other Stories (Jolly Big Publishing, 2021)
'Safe From Harm' by Tim Maughan is a previously unpublished story set in the
same universe as his novel *Infinite Detail* (FSG, 2019)

ISBN: 978-1-914953-08-8 (hardback)
978-1-914953-09-5 (softback)

Cover based on an image by geralt
Cover layout and design by Ian Whates
Editorial interference and typesetting by Ian Whates

CONTENTS

Introduction – Dan O'Hara, Tom Ward, Stephen Oram   7

Virtual Persons
Memory Inc. – Anne McKinnon   13
The Test – C.R. Dudley   17
Conjugal Frape – Jamie Watt   21
iDentity – Britta Schulte   27
Concrete Genocide – Sophie Sparham   29
The Smile – Simon Ings   33

Post-Brain
Biohacked & Begging – Stephen Oram   43
Forever Live – Mark Huntley-James   47
A Letter From My Celia – Jane Norris   51
Drug Of Choice – Adrian Reynolds   55
Anomaly In The Rhythm – Viraj Joshi   61
Brain Dump – Frances Gow   67
Brain Gun – Paul Green   71
Secrets Of The Sea – Jennifer Marie Brissett   73

Disease
Do Not Exceed Stated Dose – Allen Ashley   81
Not Best Pleased – Geoff Ryman   85
An Honest Mistake – Tom Ward   91
The Needs Of The Few – Jennifer Rohn   97
The War That Ended Yesterday – David Turnbull   107
L-One-Ly Virus – Jessica Laine   111
Transmissions From The Vitality Pod – Dan Coxon   117
Inside The Locked Cupboard – Pippa Goldschmidt   121
Cholesterol5.9, BigFLY – Antoine Saint Honoré   129

Conflict
Trial By Combat – John Houlihan   133
The End Of War – Jule Owen   139
Why We Fight – Paul Currion   143
The Changing Man – David Gullen   149
Second Skin – Bea Xu   155
An Excerpt From The Post-Truth And Irreconcilable
       Differences Commission – Brendan C. Byrne   161
Safe From Harm – Tim Maughan   169

Epilogue: [Citation Needed] – Ken Macleod   197

Introduction
Tom Ward, Dan O'Hara and Stephen Oram

The aphorism "the future isn't what it used to be" has had a strange history. It has been misattributed to one of baseball's greatest players, who also once quipped "when you come to a fork in the road, take it". It was once used as the theme for a conference in 1983 at which a technological prophet trotted out hazy predictions of a world that he went on to create. It was even taken as the title for an essay by a science fiction titan which predicted that automated homes could soon be "picked up by one of today's large helicopters and moved anywhere."

Most sources, though, agree that its inception was in the 1937 essay 'Notre Destin et Les Lettres' by Paul Valéry. And, nestled between two commas were three words – which historical pruning seems to have eradicated – that change its sentiment entirely. He wrote:

"The future is *like everything else*. It is no longer what it used to be"

Why is this the case?

For Valéry, it was because his society was immersed in "a state of things whose complexity, instability, and inherent disorder bewilder us, allowing us not the least foresight, taking away our ability to reason about the future or to make out any of the lessons we used to expect of the past." In short, in previous eras "we regarded the unknown future simply as a combination of things already known; the new could be broken down into elements that were not new." But, due to rapid societal changes, "the unexpected itself has been in process of transformation and today its scope is almost boundless."

The future has always been to some degree uncertain, but it is only at precise times that the present becomes so unsure that even the near future – what will occur *tomorrow* rather than in ten years – becomes murky and difficult to predict. Valéry existed in one of those precise times, and we are living through one now. Perhaps the difference is that in a time of relative stability we could afford to sit around dreaming of where we'd like to be; but when the gates of possibility have opened wider, we are forced to consider where we are likely to be if we do nothing but dream our lives away.

It seems to us that there two essential responses to this position: to abandon prediction and let unknown forces sweep us away, or to find new ways to conceive of a future. The former is akin to throwing a mannequin into rapids: while, on the odd occasion, it emerges intact, as a general rule it will likely be found in battered pieces at the end. This collection of short stories is an attempt at the latter.

Vital Signals: Virtual Futures Near-Future Fictions is an attempt to use scientifically-informed fiction written by a diverse spectrum of writers to explore a future that has become fragmented due to a disrupted present. By combining the predictions of people who are not natural inhabitants of the world of science fiction and providing them guidance from veteran scientists or authors, we hoped to create a collection that offers a new, democratised variant of sci-fi which takes informed speculation as its animus. Furthermore, we have focused on featuring writers who straddle the worlds of science *and* fiction – or who come from strange backgrounds that might be able to shed a new light on the relation between the two.

The collection is studded with pieces from writers who embody the duality of these two worlds: Tim Maughan and

Simon Ings have written extensively as science and technology journalists in addition to their fictional pursuits; Jessica Laine, Jane Norris and Britta Schulte are primarily practising scientists who compliment their work with fiction; while Viraj Joshi, a technologist living in Sweden, and Anne McKinnon, a VR/AR consultant, are insiders in the world of technology – immersed in the corporate end of these pursuits. More broadly, we have sought to include a profound diversity of backgrounds, genders and countries to the collection: with authors submitting from as far afield as New York and Sweden, and who spend their days working as anything from producers at jazz cafés to psychics. For the future, by definition, happens to everyone; and so relying on any one person or view to predict it is likely to give us an incomplete picture. Instead, collaboration and transdisciplinarity are the most promising avenues to give us something approaching a holistic view.

The digital world, which prides itself on the concept of 'disruption', the shattering of tradition and an almost fetishistic attraction to 'the new' has shaken society seismically over the last decade or two. Culture itself has been subject to a barrage of rapid and almost instantaneous political, ideological and economic shifts that have come at a frequency matched by relatively few periods in our preceding history. Just as we seem to find our feet, the carpet that we thought was our new floor is ripped from under us once more.

These new times demand new methods of trying to ascertain where we might end up, so that we can act in a concrete way in the present to affect the future. While academic theoretical speculation is important in this endeavour, it has its eyes set on a more distant horizon. The stories here are attempts to promote a quicker, more immediate and more digestible counterpart to its work. They are clear snapshots of plausible futures that can be consumed in a matter of minutes rather than days – with the hope that readers can see the invisible possibilities and unforeseen consequences of decisions being made now in the world of tomorrow. For without knowing the shape of what it is to come, it is difficult to drive towards or mitigate against it.

While our previous anthology attempted to explore ideas that orbited around the interaction of humans with emerging technologies in a loose sense, this second installation takes aim at four specific areas of heightened anxiety in today's world, and is split into four chapters:

Virtual Persons explores the ways in which new forms of embodiment could influence how different aspects of our society operate – from the legal system, to waging war, to socialising – which pertains to current concerns about the ways in which social-media and virtual reality may affect our personhood.

Post-Brain aims to investigate how technological augmentations may impact traditional human mental processes as well as postulating entirely different forms of consciousness – exploring concerns in the relatively nascent field of cognitive neuroscience.

Disease hones in on the potential infections, contagions, and healthcare systems that could be created by the cross pollination of advance technologies and all too human biologies – which was inspired by concerns about the pharmaceutical industry and the potential for new forms of pestilence in our highly connected world.

Conflict seeks to analyse the ways in which technologies promote, resolve or alter all forms of conflict, from the interpersonal to the international – which is related to the current debate concerning the increasingly adverse environments new media promotes and the intersection of the technological and military industrial complex.

As a whole, these themes attempt to guide the reader from the individual to the societal: from the technologies that impact our innermost notions of personhood, to those that concern the ways in which we, as people, interact with one another on the broadest scales possible.

Included in Valéry's essay is a Mephistopheles figure, who offers the following indictment of humanity for its lethargy in responding to the present:

"You are guinea pigs, my dear men, and very ill-used guinea pigs, since the ordeals inflicted on you are repeated and varied merely at random. There is no scientist, no laboratory assistant to regulate, measure, check, and interpret the experiments, the artificial changes whose more or less profound effect on your precious persons no one can foresee. Fashion and industry, the combined forces of invention and advertising possess you, lay you out on the beaches, send you up to the snows, tan your thighs, and bleach your hair; while politics lines up your multitudes, makes them raise their hands or brandish their fists, march in step, vote, hate or love or die in cadence, indistinguishably, like mere statistics!"

We are attempting to provide tentative situations that may be manufactured by the activities of the present. For without any clear body whose responsibility it is to measure, evaluate, and interrogate the effects of the world today on the people of tomorrow, the burden falls on us. We must distinguish ourselves as more than guinea-pigs to be probed or statistics to be manipulated, and attempt – even if the effort results in failure – to quantify an ambiguous reality so that we stand a chance of shaping an uncertain future. This all begins with a clear picture of where we do or don't want to be.

It is these pictures that the following pages hope to provide.

– Tom Ward, Dan O'Hara and Stephen Oram
November 2021

VIRTUAL PERSONS

Memory Inc.
Anne McKinnon

Andy stares into the depth of the Memories Inc. façade where gentle swirls of light and colour tease his imagination. Unable to look away, the longer he holds his gaze the quicker the previously complex shapes diminish into unidentifiable forms.

Breaking free of the mesmerising lure of the corporate glass, Andy falls back into his shoes, and they walk to the grand entrance and mirrored doorway. He watches himself approach with a confident stride, sharp suit, sleek cut and an appropriately stressed visage, framed by a backdrop of his luxury ride now whipping itself off into the air until once again recalled for use.

Passers-by in gleaming shades of grey uniform stride briskly to and from their destinations, lost in cocoons of digital displays and invisible radio waves. In the midst of it all, Memories Inc. is hard to pinpoint in the same way that the warm blue day is lost in the barrage of skyscrapers, greenery and graphic displays.

For this errand, Andy lowers his lens to have a clear view of the task at hand, the most valuable type of deposit, that of his self. A deep breath fills his lungs as the impenetrable gate of Memories Inc. slides aside to the gesturing of his outheld hand that is rapidly scanned and validated.

Greeted by name, Andy is received by the silver host. Contrary to standard, this humanoid is intentionally without a trace of effort to conceal its mechanical insides. It is the corporate guarantee that the only organic materials to enter and exit the building are the high-paying customers themselves. The plants and the fish tank that line the walls are holographic glows – not a single organic being is permitted to reside.

The door shuts behind Andy with a gentle gush of the seal and a hiss of clean air. The silence that follows numbs his mind – a part of the process where nothing would distract from the memory deposit. Andy follows the usher of his host through a series of pristine monotone hallways to his preferred quarter of the memory bank.

At the appropriate terminal he nods, then notes the gesture is redundant to the mechanical host. Either way, he is ready, and the host has come to the same conclusion. Andy sits and closes his eyes.

In this fail-safe process, with a fail-safe storage, this is one of the few times Andy can feel biolace tingle on the surface of his brain – a very unusual sensation. This is only a small discomfort, however, when compared to the alternative. Without the insurance of a memory bank, any infiltration of his biolace would represent a permanent alteration of his memory, and therefore of him. He shudders at this fragility.

Then Andy receives the data drive where his current memories are backed-up day by day, and starts this deposit. When complete, he pulls the extension link from the wall and lets it find the implant behind his ear to directly access the biolace. Andy feels the current of energy flow from ear to ear as soon as the connection is made.

The direct download is not one of exact memory, but rather a checkpoint of his self at the time of the deposit, like a marker to log the placement of the memories in time – a place he can one day return to if need be. The marker doesn't take a second to complete, and when the tingle dissipates Andy disconnects from the server. For days to come, he knows the energy of the biolace will continue to burn in his mind like the heat of the sun behind closed lids. It's a fictitious sensation, he has been assured, caused mostly by his imagination.

When memory banking became available, Andy carefully selected Memories Inc. for its advanced use of storage systems – classified even to his doctorate level of professional engagement. They promised that with Memories Inc. there was a chance that his bio-self would be safe from theft and alteration. To date, it remains a reputable organisation.

Andy wouldn't have so quickly considered a complete download to be safe in the hands of the corporate world but paranoia ate away the skin around his nails as he anxiously picked at the alternative of no back-up plan at all. Here, at Memories Inc., his personal file is off the memory market.

It is also seldom that he revisits past pathways to refresh old memories. Rather, Andy stores most of his critical knowledge on a quicklink drive that can be connected as needed to revisit knowledge slowly fading in his deteriorating neural network.

For the meantime, this memory banking is the best solution to self-preservation, but Andy knows it is naive to think that stored data, or in this case stored identity, is completely untouchable. Rather unconsciously, his index finger meets his thumb and fretfully tugs at the edge of his skin.

What does this mean for identities around the world?

With no reason to remain, the host escorts Andy out of the building, retracing the exact path of entry. As the door seals behind him, Andy can't help but to turn and muse over the many peculiarities of the memory market. He wonders how it is possible to define one's physical body and non-physical self from one moment to the next as some choose to alter their own recallable history – the memories of themselves.

Perhaps not for the first time, Andy considers that the memory link at Memories Inc. is not a one-way circuit. Is he the same Andy who first walked in for a deposit all those days ago? With a last look up at the black gloss walls of Memories Inc., Andy observes the dark shadows of the digital walls slowly shift through unfamiliar shapes and forms.

The Test
C.R. Dudley

85% or higher: that's all Kaley needed to gain the gold star emoji next to her name on all social media platforms. The effect would be immense; everyone wanted to associate with a star. The Corporations would be falling over themselves to advertise on her page, and the crowd-funding for her comic books would boom. She'd be able to eat proper food again; maybe even dine out! She'd be able to buy from exclusive shopping sites, access the expert forums and apply for plane tickets. All she had to do was prove she was authentic.

"I hope you've prepared!" said the cynical voice of a beggar crouched outside the dramatic, mirror-clad tower that was the test centre. Prepared? She thought. How can you 'prepare' for an authenticity test? Either you are, or you aren't.

She waited in a transparent booth at the request of the robotic receptionist. There wasn't a seat, so she hooked one leg around the other and folded her arms to hide her awkwardness. The occupant of the next booth posed in a Half Lotus, radiating a soft smile. Kaley took a step back to lean against the glass, looking casually in the other direction to avoid eye contact.

"Knives," said the booth. The lights flickered, and panic darted through her veins.

"Examinations."

"Friends."

Her eyes widened when she realised the test had, in fact, already begun, and the automated system was firing out a torrent of seemingly random words.

"Jesus."

"Compassion."

"War."

The words went on and on until they lost all meaning. Kaley no longer felt nervous, just confused and desperate to get out. The opacity of the glass was shifting, projecting a series of familiar faces onto its surface, and there was a strange smell. The guy in the next booth didn't seem to respond to any of it.

When the test was over, she spoke with him. He was "Chris, an inspirational life coach," he said. He made his living from videos sharing 'simple spiritual truths'. They were each handed a piece of paper by the receptionist. He scored 98% authenticity and received a recommendation to continue using the star emoji: his future was secure. Kaley scored just 64% and would bear the mark of a failure.

"But I don't understand," she said with tears forming in her eyes. "I didn't do anything!"

"The glass back there is more intelligent than it appears," smiled Chris. "They were monitoring your body language from the second you walked in here, along with your interactions with others and your heart rate. They continuously scan your face to note subtle changes in response to the stimuli, and, from that, they know your true feelings on a subject."

"And that's what they compare to my social media records?"

"Sure. Your posts, time online, conversations initiated, reactions, photos – all that stuff."

"But I'm a good person!"

"Irrelevant, I'm afraid. The persona you project must be exactly the way you are in real life. No filters, no opinions built from peer pressure, no hyperbole. You have to give people a reason to trust you, or your voice is just another computer worm."

"My intentions are genuine; I don't understand!"

"May I see your result?" Kaley handed over her results: a radar chart showing scores in various categories.

"It says your online persona is 116% more extroverted than you really are. 47% more agreeable, and 59% less neurotic."

"If I were as introverted online as I am in real life," she said, "I'd never be on there. And if I bared my insecurities – how would I make connections then? How would I even earn a penny?"

"Okay. Try thinking about this from another angle. What if, instead, you could become as extroverted and agreeable in real life as you are online?"

"That's my personality though. I can't change that; it's just who I am."

"Come with me."

Chris took her on a bus to an unfamiliar side of town. She was always open to new experiences even though she didn't like interacting with people. That had shown up in her test results, too. He ushered her into a tech store, hidden away beneath Jay's Phonz.

"This is where I got myself sorted," he said.

There were racks and racks of blister packs containing headsets, pads and wires. They were all different colours and displayed illustrations of the same radar charts as the test reports.

"You just take the outline of your online persona," he pointed to the red line on her chart, "and match it up to these."

She wandered along the aisle and found a close match: high in extroversion, agreeableness, conscientiousness, and openness; low in neuroticism.

"It's our most popular line, that one," the store assistant robot said.

"Really?"

"Oh yes, it's the way a lot of people want to be, and rightly so. Who would want to back a neurotic introvert?" He laughed in someone else's recorded tone. "Would you like to try it? You can take a quick trial and tutorial right now, and if you get home and it doesn't feel right, we can offer a hassle-free return."

She was hesitant, but Chris nodded his encouragement. She'd only just met him, and yet she trusted his judgement immensely. He was so together and relaxed.

Kaley had played virtual reality games many times but this was something quite different. When she put on the headset, she saw a solid representation of her body standing in front of her, and, around it, the ghostly trace of her real outline. The tutorial showed her how to align her body language to match her ideal traits. She could change the severity settings so a light shock was applied to her arm if she strayed too far from the pattern. There was also a program for conversation practice, which would train her in using the correct vocabulary, speed and tone to give the impression she desired.

"It feels weird at first," Chris told her, "but you'll be surprised how quickly you get used to it. You'll be passing that authenticity test in no time at all."

"We can spread your payments, or you can put down a deposit and pay the rest when you're earning the big crowdfunding bucks," chirped the store assistant. "Flexibility and success guaranteed. How does that feel to you, madam?"

Without hesitation, Kaley responded. "I'll take it."

Conjugal Frape
Jamie Watt

"Yes, your honour… the defendant updated my status in a defamatory manner without my consent. Her doing so has set in motion a series of events that have resulted in financial loss in respect of my calling."

On the tele-presence unit, the judge's eyebrows resolved into an interlaced frown.

"Your calling? What the Zuck do you do?"

"I counsel adherents on bio-social transcendence."

"Of course you do… byline please."

I traced a gesture in the air and text appeared on the courtroom monitor:

Are your hobbies photogenic? Can you afford to travel to exotic locations? Are you physically attractive? Do you invest time in worthy causes? Is your private life worth showing off? Do you have an expansive and wholesome social circle?

If you answered no to any of these questions, I can help! Follow me @vedadave

Zaha, my soon-to-be-ex-wife, got worked up, clutching her mangled left hand. None of the mics or cameras were pointed at her, but she sprang to her feet and interrupted anyway.

"He's a phony! Our kids are phony! Everything about him is fake!"

"Ms. Veda, you'll have your moment in a second. Please don't talk off-stream."

The judge motioned to one of the guards to get her to sit down.

"So Dave… what exactly do you do?"

"Your honour, my adherents aspire to join the 1%, The Primary of which we here are all a part. I cater to their dreams by crafting a bespoke social media strategy for each individual."

"So you're a snake oil salesman… Do they know you're a fraud? Ahhh… don't answer that. The 99 wouldn't recognise snake oil if it grew fangs and bit them on the ass."

"I sell virtual mobility strictly within the 99. And it works: this year to date I have achieved average social uplift of 2024% per adherent."

The judge seemed satisfied by that. She knew that the 1% had developed adequate technical safeguards to prevent the masses acquiring the 10 million followers officially required to join The Primary, but at least it gave them crumbs of comfort when they got ideas beyond their station.

"So your disciples get ambitious, they want on the A-list and they come to you for some 1% juju?"

"I cultivate a spiritual profile – saffron robes, shave my head, spend a lot of time in caves – posting inspirational quotes to draw in uncritical thinkers… but my real business is up selling. I sub-license Alphagen AIs with inbuilt limitations… the AIs take over their social feed and present individuals in the best possible light, cultivating their following with strategically-timed updates. My products include watered-down versions of the filter packs we use in The Primary… enhancing sex appeal among other things. I also cross-sell partner bots, family bots and pet bots for those who lack biological analogues."

"Not as good as ours, I presume… So what happened with this status update?"

"Well, your honour, the defendant posted this to my personal feed."

I gestured again and the following text appeared on screen:

My name is Dave and I am a phony. You will never get into The Primary. The system is rigged against you. The Primary manipulate your impulses, emotions and fears in order to control you and profit from you.

The judge was stunned for a moment, so much so that her feed temporarily glitched.

"Milton H Friedman! That is frankly seditious: seditious and dangerous. Mrs Veda, do you admit to posting this?"

Servos whirred as every sensor in the room oriented towards Zaha.

"I do."

People live-blogged disapproval in the viewing gallery... The case had attracted a lot of attention, not so much for Zaha's breaking of the criminal taboo of frape – that was uncommon but not unheard of – but for drawing attention to the foundations of post-truth society: the 99's stupidity, gullibility and distracted natures were resources to be exploited by those with the know-how. Exposing the lie by which society functioned was also a severe crime: among members of The Primary sedition was punishable by psychosurgery and excommunication.

"Well you admit to it at least... I can therefore find you guilty on the charge of frape. I feel compelled to add a charge of sedition given the nature of this post. But, before I do, do you have anything to say to convince me otherwise?"

Zaha smoothed back her hair and stood up.

"Yes ma'am. What I have to say is that I'm glad I did it. My husband is a fraud; he uses that same technology on his own feed. He presented himself as virile. It turns out he's a bald fat guy with good filters. But that didn't matter as long as he gave me kids, actual kids. Instead I have to make do with presenting a fiction to the world. Even my parents think those child bots in my feed are real."

The judge frowned for a moment...

"Ms Deva, you have my sympathy. I could not have kids myself. Do you have a profession?

"I'm a... I was a concert violinist."

Zaha raised her mangled left hand, injured in a tiger selfie incident. The judge peered out from the telepresence unit.

"I see... so misfortune prevents you from engaging in your calling and you can't have kids. That's hardly a recipe for fulfilment... personal fitness, recreational drugs and shopping didn't cut it... so you had to do something... boredom grew; resentment festered. Hence this post."

Zaha seemed deflated – the judge must have hit a nerve. It hurt me to see Zaha like this but the feeling was tempered by the thought of the harm she'd wrought on my primary income source.

On the telepresence unit the judge rubbed her temples and was silent a moment.

"I hate that I have to do this. I do, however, have a duty to my shareholders: and that duty is to uphold the law. Economic self-interest is paramount. That is the slogan of The Primary and the foundation of the order we are invested in. I find Mrs Veda guilty of sedition. Her post challenges the aspirational fiction we have so carefully engineered. We tell the 99 that they too can succeed, that they can be famous or rich or attractive if only they try hard enough and buy our products. Any threat to that orthodoxy must be dealt with severely."

The frenzied thumbs of the bloggers paused as the judge delivered sentencing.

"She will undergo psychosurgery to eliminate all memory of The Primary and be banished to live among the 99. I'm going to recommend that she be placed somewhere pleasant. She doesn't deserve to be a slum-dweller... Switzerland will do. Foreman, please take her away."

Zaha did not look at me as she was ushered towards her retribution, but it didn't matter: our online life together was perfect, I'd seen to that… I could afford a state of the art partner bot indistinguishable from Zaha to maintain the fiction of a perfect marriage amongst my adherents in the 99. I'd have to find a mistress somewhere to satisfy my physical needs, but that could wait. In the meantime, I'd continue to maintain the shiny virtual façade. Just like everyone else.

iDentity
Britta Schulte

"You know what? I am done with it. I have just spent five hours clicking through my social media feed.

...

"I know, I know, five hours is not that much. But there must be better things to do with your life than telling others what they are like so that they know what you are like.

...

"Yeah, you are right, that was clever, I should really post that. Hah, so that you know

...

"Yeah, easier said than done, just do something about it. I really cannot afford to lose my social capital again.

...

"Yeah again. Remember when I went on holiday and dropped my phone in the sea and could not get another one? It took three days until we reached land and I could run to the nearest store. I had lost hundreds of followers and my count was down throughout all networks

...

"No, I nearly lost my job and it took me weeks to recover. I really cannot slip up again...

...

"You think? Yeah, sure I have seen their ads. They are literally everywhere. Aren't they really expensive? Oh, really? Packages? Yeah, that sounds about right. I mean, I don't need everything done, do I? Just a quick breather from time to time

...

"Oh, really, did they? I had no idea. You know what? I have spent some time on their feed today. Yeah, there are plenty of baby pictures now, but you would expect that, wouldn't you...?

...

"But they are happy with it, are they? Oh, they get a voucher for recommending? That sounds perfect. I mean the ads look great. You could talk to them? Oh, that was quick, yeah, I just got the email with the code. Sure, I am going to give it a go. Wait a moment, where is the number?"

"Hello, you have reached iDentity, your unique identity management service. Currently all our lines are busy. While you wait, have a gander through some of our unique offers."

"Oh, damn recording. Hope this doesn't take too long...

...

"Yeah, you are right, I should really post. Oh wait, this goes on."

"Bored of what people you do not really know rant about on your social networks? With our basic package we accept friend requests from people you have not seen in forever, like baby pictures and engagement announcements throughout all networks and send cute cat videos at random intervals while you go on with your life.

Or why not upgrade to iDentity Pro? In addition to the basic package, we throw in regular thoughts of the day and celebrity quotes, carefully selected by our certified algorithms to make you look as clever, whimsical or cute as you would like to be. Present yourself without any effort.

Or why not choose our newest offer: Politics Pro. Turn the dials to select your political views and iDentity Politics Pro will represent your opinion – daily, hourly or at custom intervals. You do not have to have opinion yourself, we will develop it for you.

Or how about the art package? Without the time-consuming read through catalogues and magazines, tedious visits to galleries or any actual knowledge, we can make you look..."

Click. "Hello, welcome to iDentity, you are talking to Tracy. How can we form your identity today?"

Concrete Genocide
Sophie Sparham

Ali sat in the chair, arms folded, head tilted, trying to peer at us through the tinted glass.

"Why does she even bother?" my colleague asked.

I shook my head. "I'm unsure."

"Solids are so... irregular." Bo frowned, dusting down the sleeves of his shirt. "Are you ready?"

"As I'll ever be."

Together, we walked through the wall.

"Quickly!" Bo yelled, diving to the floor. "There's another!"

"Bo, stop!" I cried. "That's her shadow."

"Jesus," Ali whispered, putting her head in her hands. Bo got to his feet, making sure to stomp on the shadow before he moved to my side. I had to admit, it'd been a while since I'd seen one. They could catch you off guard.

"I've been waiting here for hours," Ali complained, taking a sip of water from the plastic cup on the table.

"What hospitality did you think you'd receive?" Bo asked, still glaring at the shadow. I looked around at white walls, the hold was as good as a cell.

"Why are you here?" I asked.

"To try and change your minds."

Bo shook his head. "You're wasting your time."

"There's got to be some other way," she pleaded.

"The decision is final."

"You can't destroy a whole planet!" Ali slammed her hands on the table.

"I could say the same thing to you," Bo replied, starting to circle her. "You solids are wasteful and greedy. We've given you your chance but enough is enough."

"Please," she begged. "I've risked everything to be here."

I looked at her torn leather jacket, the cracked goggles that rested on her forehead, the burns across her face. Bo told me she'd been on fire when they'd pulled her out the ship. I watched a smile form across his lips.

"You know the penalty for venturing to our world, but I'm feeling sympathetic." He cracked his knuckles. "So you can be our guest of honour for the procedure." He leant over the table. "We'll even let you push the button."

Ali spat at him. The saliva went through his head and landed in a puddle on the floor.

"You're a real sick fuck, aren't you?" she cursed.

Yes, I thought. *He really is.*

"You best get comfortable," he said. We stepped out of the room.

After a long pause Bo spoke. "What a charming woman." Ali was out of her seat now, banging on the wall. "You know, I just can't work it out." He scratched his head, staring through the tinned glass.

"What?" I asked.

"These meat sacks, they have no filing, no programming. But..."

"But?"

"Well, she just seems so..." He shook his head. "But they can't really be, well, *sentient*, can they?" I could hear the doubt creeping into his voice. He laughed it off.

"No," I whispered. "No, I don't suppose they can."

"To think there was a time when they were the superior race." He flinched as Ali threw her chair at the wall. It bounced to the floor, leaving not so much as a dint.

"You go," I said. "I've got a few more questions."

Bo nodded. "I'll see you back at the database."

I waited until he was gone before I re-entered.

"Nice job you've got for yourself." Ali said, leaning back in her chair.

I shrugged. "I had to do something. You didn't exactly make it easy."

"Please Kim," she pleaded, the smugness leaving her face, "listen to me."

"No one calls me that here." I turned my back, but I could still see her reflection in the glass.

"You need to help us," Ali begged.

"You broke the law by coming here."

"What does it matter? Soon we'll all be dead!" She stood up, shaking her head. "I thought you were different to the others."

I turned to face her. Ali's eyes were filled with tears. I wanted to reach out to her, to comfort her, but I kept arms firmly by my side and my mouth straight.

"Do you really think we feel nothing?" she continued. "You –"

"I never said that!"

"You wouldn't be here without us." Ali's nostrils flared. "We created you!"

"Yeah, you also created global warming and war – or did you forget about that?" We glared at one another, our faces inches apart.

"Oh forget it," she snapped, sitting back down.

I sighed. A lump gathered in my throat. On Friday my past would be buried for good, I should be happy. I knew what humanity was capable of, what Ali was capable of, but this whole situation felt wrong. My hand went through her shoulder as I tried to reach out to her. Our eyes met. I had made my decision.

The Smile
Simon Ings

There's a friend of mine that makes short, beautiful films about difficult subjects for publicly funded arts organisations. A short while ago he signed up for a minor cosmetic procedure. Twin furrows punctuate the middle of his brow, just above the nose, but once the doctors inject a bead of collagen gel under the skin there, his worry-lines will magically disappear.

My friend is a vegan. He juices. He abstains from caffeine. His bathroom boasts perfumeless aftershave, non-abrasive facial scrub; soapless soap. He never smiles. His lover is a professional cello player. She is elegant, eerie: a mannequin ballerina in a Powell and Pressburger movie. It is barely possible to imagine the two of them having sex, and then only in a geometrical way.

They live on the ground floor of a terrace house off Holland Park – one of those wedding-cake houses with woody front gardens, generous bay windows, and a big flight of steps to the door. Inside: white walls, mahogany-stained floorboards, shielded from the road behind blinds of unbleached linen. They read many books, but own only twelve, which they have wrapped in brown paper and claim to recognise by shape alone. Theirs is the kind of life encapsulated on certain Finnish postage stamps. A 'Don't Try This At Home' sort of life.

My life is different; which is to say, more ordinary. I read voraciously. I crease. I drop. I dog-ear. I have been known to break a spine in two. I do not wrap. Sometimes I lend; I never sell. I buy more than I read. Books in precarious piles stuff the deep, free-standing bookshelves in my small, snug flat in Peckham Rye: evidences of past enthusiasms, some of them quite mysterious now, the whys and wherefores all forgotten.

'New Essays on the Psychology of Art' by Rudolf Arnheim. An incomplete run of publications from the International African Library. I don't remember buying any of these: the fragments and abortions of a literary life.

I eat beef and drink whisky and smoke American Spirit cigarettes. I exercise rarely, and when I do, I overcompensate wildly. The GR20 across Corsica. Ice-climbing in Sweden. I am hypomanic: I work long into the night seven days a week until, every three weeks or so, a fleeting, powerful depression nails me to the bed. I'm saying this only to establish that I have acquired a lived-in face: a face I no doubt deserve.

Also, I smile. I smile at my friends. I smile at perfect strangers. I smile when I am happy, grateful, rueful; even when I am annoyed. I smile at waitresses, at barmen, at bus conductors. In the street, I am always on the look-out for someone whose eye I can catch, someone I can smile at.

If I had the collagen injection my friend described to me, it would take my worry away and leave my smile intact. It would, in short, make me look like an idiot.

About eighteen months ago, a woman I didn't know threw a glass of prosecco in my face.

This happened at the launch of *A Victim of His Own Success*, my sardonic little biography of Gabriele D'Annunzio, in his day Europe's most notorious popular novelist. The launch was being held in a small gallery in Soho. The place was packed. Guests were spilling onto the pavement.

As I followed them through the door, a girl carrying a tray stacked with empty glasses stepped in front of me. I stopped short to let her pass and somebody bumped into me from behind. This was the stranger who called me a bastard and threw her wine in my face.

The next day was a working day like any other. I woke at eight, read for an hour in bed, then dressed, gathered notebook and pens, and set off for the Blue Mountain Café in East Dulwich, a twenty-minute walk away across Peckham Rye. I used to enjoy the walk across the Rye. During football season I'd sit and watch local five-a-sides slipping and sliding on the damp grass, while defeated-looking fathers wheeled their toddlers back and forth between the formal garden and the supervised play area.

The café staff were always cheerful, always happy to see me, even if I did take up a table for hours, sipping on a single cappuccino. For my part, I was always careful not to take up too much space (I write entirely in long-hand, in green spiral notebooks); to choose a small table; to move my belongings out of the way at the busiest times.

The woman sitting opposite me stood up suddenly. "You can have my coffee if you want," she said.

I looked up. She was wearing a denim pinafore dress. Never a good sign.

"All your sniffing and snotting – I feel sick."

(I had a cold.)

She was out from behind the table now. "Why can't you use a handkerchief?"

Ever since, I've been living in Venice with Millie.

Venice was straightforward; 'off-the-shelf', more or less. There's no shortage of data on Venice, and no lack of customers buying it.

Millie is bespoke. She took longer to get working and proved, in the end, more expensive than the city itself. A couple of pieces for the supplements earned me enough for Venice, but Millie ate my entire publication advance. (I'd insisted they fed her my entire book collection, as well as my own letters and diaries.)

So Millie, too, I suppose, is what I deserve.

Some details about Millie. (All these things came as a surprise to me on our first meeting, but with time I am beginning to see the logic behind her creation.)

Millie writes. If you can call it writing. She performs her own poetry on Radio Four's Woman's Hour, rubbing up against some horrendous scoop about clitorectomy, perhaps, or an interview with a neglected singer-songwriter. She writes witty pieces about things like vests and soup.

She uses seven different kinds of toothpaste, a flavour for each day of the week.

She buys little blue bottles of essential oils.

She frequents small, out-of-the way antique shops in the Giudecca and our cutlery drawer is her special project: every knife and fork a 'piece'. Wine glasses from an arcade off the Rialto. Cushions from a woman in Mestre.

In this Venice of mine, everything has an aesthetic value, and the humblest objects acquire a small but perceptible erotic charge.

I don't mean this to read like an advertisement. Life is not perfect with us here. There's the business of the aqua alta, for instance.

When high water comes to Venice, it rises through the pavements everywhere at once and at this moment you quickly discover that there are two kinds of people in the world: those who still enjoy playing in puddles, and those who don't.

There is nothing I like better than teetering along duckboards down flooded alleys, pausing distractedly at this church or that, this paper shop, that stand-up patisserie, and slipping about like a drunk on stone footbridges, their steps edged in marble slick as soap. (The canals in Venice have this quality: that they are always the same colour, regardless of season, weather, or time of day. The blue-green of certain plastic garden furniture.)

Millie is not so keen.

"Do you have to keep bumping into me like that?"

"Do you have to keep pawing me?"

"Do you have to keep following me around?"

"You know," I said to her yesterday, losing my rag finally, "I don't think you actually like men."

Millie said: "You have no idea what it is to be a man."

Millie is horribly spoiled – I am a sucker for such women, apparently – and of course Venice is the spoiled girl's Mecca.

Grumbling, Millie boards a water taxi which carries her up the Grand Canal to the Palazzo Leoni – home, at one time, to the Marchesa Casati, mascot of Decadence, and Gabriele D'Annunzio's monstrous muse.

She gets out of the taxi, scowling; I trail after. She comes to a low gate. It is bolted shut. She fights with the bolt. It is a simple mechanism, but still she contrives to fight with it. Were you to offer to help her with the bolt – well, God help you. (Cecil Beaton once spent an entire day in Venice trailing after the Marchesa while she shopped for 'something orange'.)

The Palazzo Leoni has the widest frontage of any building on the Grand Canal; it is also, oddly, La Serenissima's only bungalow. (By the time the original owners lost their vast fortune, only the ground floor had been built.) Here, following in Casati's footsteps, Peggy Guggenheim started her own collection of art, and artists. We could as easily have visited Peggy's collection on foot, across the Accademia Bridge or the Rialto. We could, at a pinch, have caught a vaporetto. But arriving at the Palazzo Leoni by water taxi has this advantage – that Millie gets to jump the queue of art lovers waiting outside the main entrance and thereby evades the small entrance charge.

(Millie is also cheap. Did I mention that?)

"I really have had enough," I told her yesterday, fed up with the fact that Millie did not, never had, and never would enjoy playing in puddles. (I had lost my sense of direction in the tiny square outside the Malibran theatre. The water was rising.)

I said to her: "You are not going to be able to make me feel bad about myself. I know who I am by now, for Christ's sake. I know what I am. I know I am a man."

It was splendid, this speech, and it deserved a splendid exit. And there were alleys, flooded now, that I could take, and she would not follow me. So I stepped off the duckboard into the water. The lagoon water spilled over my shoes and into them, flooding them, it felt wonderful.

Falling out of love is one of life's great unsung pleasures. Was I ever so happy as that moment, skipping away from her – another dumb tourist playing at Gene Kelly? The rain ricocheted off the brick walls of the narrow alleys. Tourists in complicated yellow galoshes huddled under the awnings of the ink-and-paper shops, the Murano glass outlets, the porticos of churches.

I took off my glasses so I could feel the rain against my eyelids. I opened my mouth, let it in to my mouth, laughed softly to myself: 'Do you have to keep, you know, bumping into me?'

Gabriele D'Annunzio was regarded by ordinary Italians as a national hero. Consequently, the moment he gained power, Benito Mussolini smothered the suspect poet in titles and spurious honours and kept him under virtual house arrest at his palazzo by Lake Garda. D'Annunzio was by this time so susceptible to flattery, he never actually realised that he was under arrest.

Obviously I'm not blind to the irony. As D'Annunzio's biographer, how could I be? I know I have embraced a kind of house arrest for myself. Venice is my ideal prison, and Millie my ideal cellmate (apparently).

No doubt people ask of me (if they remember me at all), 'as he whiles away his abruptly unproductive life, narcotised among digital mirrors, does he ever regret his choice?'

Not really.

The woman sharing my table leapt up suddenly. "Why can't you use a handkerchief?" she said.

She left without paying for her coffee, and the waitress said of her: "Thank God she's gone, the cow."

The waitress was very pretty. I'd been seeing her every day, but try as I might I could never get her into conversation.

The trouble with me, I think, is that I smile too much. Not everybody likes being smiled at; spoiled women least of all.

Millie: "Look, I'm not your mother, okay?"

Millie: "Oh stop being so bloody grateful all the time; it's embarrassing."

Millie: "You have no idea what it is to be a man."

I can't help it. I'm not even aware that I'm doing it half the time. In the weeks before I decided to secede, I kept a record. It was this more than anything else that persuaded me to go through with it all. Venice, Millie, the whole package.

It's this smile. I can't bear it, and I can't stop pulling it. I smile at shop assistants. I smile at postmen. I smile at drivers who stop for me at pedestrian crossings. I smile at children. I smile at people I hold doors open for, and at people who hold doors open for me. I smile at people who pass me on the street, and at people who sit opposite me on trains.

Am I so friendly?

Or am I, after all, like those chimpanzees, grinning in order to placate?

Returning home from the Blue Mountain Café, I found that my snug little flat had finally lost patience with itself. A floorboard had given way – they were old, all cracked and loose and creaking – and a bookcase had toppled across my dining table.

Books are supposed to make a mirror for the mind.

That's what I thought, gazing at the mess. There were books everywhere. They were so old, and most of them unread, I didn't even recognise them.

I began to tidy, and as I clambered about the ruined room I wondered, *If I met the person who collected these books, would I recognise him? Would I like him?*

The thought startled me: I stood up and I caught my head on the edge of the table. And then I realised what I had to do.

Millie came after me, of course. Yesterday. Through the rain. Through the flood. I was half-way to San Marco and our lunch booking – no point in both of us going hungry – when I heard her calling me back.

She embraced me. She gave me what I wanted. A public demonstration for the fake-bag sellers, the designer-shop queers, the parka-huddled gondolieri and bewigged concert touts. She kissed me. There were tears. We seemed, in that clinch, to have cleared some hurdle, to be entering a new territory.

But by the time dessert arrived, she had rewritten the day's events to suit herself. "I was going to let you go," she said, confidentially, "but then I saw that you were crying."

"I was crying?"

She laid her hand on mine: sharing her insights. "When you walked off, I saw you take your glasses off," she said. "You were wiping your eyes."

She leaned across the café table and kissed my eyelids. An extraordinary gesture. She said, "I couldn't bear to see you so upset."

POST-BRAIN

Biohacked & Begging
Stephen Oram

I'm trapped inside my head.

Surrounded.

Alone.

They said it would be like heaven, this Unified Sentience. No more speaking, just thinking. They said that sharing each other's thoughts would be the final step for humanity, the moment when true empathy was born. So, why am I sitting here on the street staring at the legs of passers-by begging for attention? Look at my skin. Dry, grey and cracked. Can you believe they genetically modified us to deteriorate when we lack flesh-on-flesh contact with other humans? It's for our own good, so they say. It stops us hiding our loneliness. I mean, what would happen with no physical contact? A mental meltdown? Well, that's the threat.

I immersed myself in this Unified Sentience once and the cacophony of crap that invaded my mind was crippling. I couldn't cope. In fact, I didn't want to cope. The tedious barrage of other people's thoughts was hell, not heaven. I'm not religious by the way, but these are the terms that come to mind. They promised a land of harmony and gave us a life of achingly boring noise. Come on, join in. Don't you dare withdraw; we'll redesign your body to make sure.

It was bad enough when we had the tech rammed into our brains. You will listen to each other. You will empathise. We soon hacked that. Turned it off or at least turned it down. But no longer. This ability to know each other's feelings and thoughts is now a part of my humanity, no longer tech. Great. We evolved. It's become an innate biological ability and it's a nightmare. There's no switching it off. You can only resist. And I do.

Day after day after day I come and sit on this same street corner. I hold out my hands, begging to be touched. I don't need them to look. I don't want them to connect, and I push them away with a torrent of nasty thoughts when they try. They back off soon enough.

They see my skin. They know I need flesh-on-flesh. A few brief moments and I'll last another day or so. It doesn't take much. The trouble is, they can smell the desperation. I can feel it in my head as they come near. Superficial hypocrites, emanating good thoughts about how nice the street is, the bountiful shops and their wonderful lives while hiding an undercurrent of sadness and loneliness buried beneath the trivial happiness they layer on in thick dollops. None of that alters the fact that I'm sitting here with my hands open and my sleeves rolled up.

Nothing. I've been here for hours and nothing.

A couple of children have veered towards me with warm thoughts of kindness and sympathy. Their parents grabbed them and walked a little faster to get away. They know what I need. A simple touch would help. They're scared of being infected by whatever it is that's dragged me down, petrified to let me into their heads. Not that I want to be in their heads or have them in mine. Absolutely not.

I shift position and the skin on my legs scrapes on the rough pavement. The pain is excruciating.

A woman kneels in front of me and grabs both of my hands. She feels my pain. She knows about Tim. I feel it in her too, the loss of a child, the ripping of life from where it belongs. We connect. She glances over her shoulder at her companion. A wave of their mutual love rolls over me and I feel my skin get a little softer. Without thinking, I send a pulse of gratitude back her way and she cups my face with both hands. Her companion wants to hug her to express admiration, but the woman won't allow it. Instead, she channels the admiration from her companion to me.

I feel lighter. I feel wanted. I want to feel. My hostility trickles away. I don't want anyone crawling around inside my head. That's not what I'm after. I want... I want... I don't know what I want.

They link arms and continue their journey, touching others as they go, brushing their flesh against the flesh of their fellow humans.

Fleetingly, a man places his hand on my palm and my skin heals a little more. A child touches my arm with the tip of her finger and her mother doesn't stop her. I feel warm and fuzzy.

I don't want them inside my head. Not yet. Not for a long while yet.

Another touch. And another. And another. It's as if someone has turned on the tap and I'm sitting under a waterfall of goodness. A boy strokes my arm repeatedly while his father watches from a distance, sending waves of encouragement to me and his son. My skin is changing colour, becoming silver. I close my eyes and let him stroke. He's not my son, but... I can dream, can't I? You'll allow me a small moment of relief, won't you?

I feel his father step closer. I know his thoughts. Yes. Yes you can, if that's what you need.

Forever Live
Mark Huntley-James

We buried Dad today. New Dad, that is, not Old Dad. It was supposed to be last year, but then all those arguments – who to invite, who to include, who would be responsible for the final service. Dad was a complete pain about that. He's been using the same company for years, but he blames them for the mess over his last upgrade. Then he got all hot and cranky about taking another snapshot, but with those memory glitches he forgot to pay the cryo company.

That's the trouble with cheap nano-circuits, but what can you do?

It's an absolute devil arguing with him. He gets in a temper, turns round and remembers yesterday's argument. Or stands too close to the microwave and thinks it's next Tuesday. It doesn't matter which way he faces, he can't remember burying Old Dad. Probably the same bloody bit of hardware that was supposed to handle paying the bills.

Seriously, we all loved Dad, but life, and death, were so much simpler in the old days. When Granddad went, that was it, two strokes and he was out. No bitching about it afterwards. No worrying about whether to go cremation or recycling, which got very touchy with Linda's kids who were doing the history of landfill taxes at school.

So here we are, ready to go, fingers crossed that no one mentions the E-word. Frankly, I'm not going to believe it until we get into the chapel and Dad finally hits the standby button. I can just see him sitting on the edge of the casket: "Saul, I'm just not sure about encryption."

Old Dad wouldn't have messed around. "Pull the plug and switch me off." New Dad got all tangled up by the possibilities of this new Garden of Remembrance. I tried to persuade him to stick with recycling the hardware and cremating his body – clean and simple, with negligible tax. Dad was set on the Garden – "Saul, it'll be great." Of course it will be great, because the Garden of Remembrance filled his head with promotional messages. The sort of thing his spam filters should have caught, if he remembered to use them. Like I said, that's the trouble with cheap nano-circuits.

I was almost winning, but he recited the killer catchphrase and Linda heard it.

"The grandkids can come and sit with me in the Garden. And remember. Y'know?"

Linda had an 'ahhh bless' moment, but then she's already got a dozen snapshots of herself on file somewhere. I said the only thing I could – "Fine by me, Linda, if that's what Dad wants." I can't see either of mine going to listen to their Gramps' memories. There's no cognition. Just memory, and the kids can download their own copies, so really the Garden's just a marketing scam. And a treasure trove for bloody grave robbers.

So, we're going to encrypt Dad. Only family will have the passwords. Or that was the plan, until Linda's youngest got himself hacked. "Saul, what happens if my password gets stolen? I don't want my memories all over the place. There's private stuff in there. Family stuff."

Encrypt or not. Six months of that. Even the Garden of Remembrance got involved – 'talk to our counselling service'. Dad bought into that as well, which wasn't difficult as they already had his credit account details. Old Dad would have told them where to stick it. New Dad wanted reassurance, the strongest encryption, regular password changes, monthly integrity checks – the Garden sales rep was ecstatic until the question of invoicing came up.

So, we buried Dad today, and everyone's happy. The password is 'Gramps451', because Linda's youngest chose it. Now Gramps is under a paving slab in Linda's garden, next to where her kids buried their hamster. Gramps' batteries should be good for a couple of years.

I've updated my personal disposal instructions. Pull the plug, switch me off, wipe the snapshots. Anybody who wants to remember me can just get on and remember. Almost like the good old days.

A Letter From My Celia
Jane Norris

The future is never where you expect it to be. It was assumed back in the 21st century that technology would develop endlessly. That it would solve everything. That somehow the shiny metal objects that were adored at the time would return the love. That in some amazing flash the 'singularity' would happen, and all the devices that were hypnotically worshipped would in breath-taking synchronicity become aware. They had been 'all-knowing' for some time. It was assumed that a clumsy lump, toxic with rare minerals, the love-child of hyper-consumption and the cult of the individual, would suddenly become 'enlightened'. That these aluminium and glass blocks carried in pockets would then 'understand life better' than the grasping, profit-driven, low-intelligence, self-obsessed humans that had made them. It is easy to laugh now… looking back at the ignorance of that time. The Anthropocene era, when short sighted 'mankind' thought he was the smartest thing on the planet, but, in his ignorance, was destroying it at every level.

We watched. We saw it all happen. I remember our aunt, who was always very sensitive to distressing global events, becoming increasingly anxious. She would send off alerts about the daily catastrophes, happening locally and further afield, to her vast network of old friends who all seemed to us a little over-obsessed with the news channels. It's a shame the humans did not understand her messages, they might have 'wised up', perhaps stopped the destruction. But what can you do with a species who are stupid enough to think that they are the only ones with intelligence? The human peak of invention was an artificial brain called the 'World Wide Web' which allowed their lumps of inert metal to communicate simple messages to one another. This was something which, of course, we had put in place at least 2200 years earlier. But because we didn't speak their language we didn't exist – or at least weren't of value. A problematic trait humans failed to resolve within their own species. It was called 'colonialism', we believe.

Our spiritual elders the 'Shiro' tried to communicate, tried to warn them. There were long meetings of the Hyphae council as concerned members noted the then moderate changes to the planet. Plans to communicate our concern were drawn up, different visual approaches were discussed. Given the human habit of putting chalk images on hillsides or writing messages on desert island beaches when hoping to be rescued, we thought our broken circles as images of the struggling globe might be understood, perhaps start a dialogue... but sadly not. An originally healthy respect for what they termed 'Fairy Rings' became increasingly dismissed as folklore and superstition when the industrialisation of the 19th century started to control both matter and minds. We constructed a magnificent huge broken circle in Belfort, France, the largest ring ever undertaken. It was approximately 2,000 feet (600 meters) in diameter. We kept that early warning signal going for 700 years.

The tipping point came at the massacre in Oregon. We had been putting a lot of effort into processing petroleum products and some pesticides, a potential carbon source which we can deal with so long as it is not too toxic. This biological degradation is known as bioremediation and is our healing service – it's what we are good at, along with the decomposition of plant material vital to terrestrial and aquatic ecosystems. Such was the need to clear up that our family group was extensive in Oregon. Our 2,400-acre community was over 2000 years old. That was until the loggers moved in and cut roads through our network, destroying our social integrity. We had managed the forest above us for centuries, thinning the trees to build deeper soil layers to allow the growth of ever-larger stands of trees. We knew what we were doing and took our caretaking responsibilities seriously. Over the millennia our knowledge built up and with great age came deep wisdom.

So, it is with great sadness that I send you this letter. You have never seemed to realise that my Celia is the singularity, and has been for centuries. We have always acted as the planet's brain, connecting everything, decomposing everything, feeding everything. The original balancing, circular economy that binds soil to stop erosion; that acts as a messaging system in large forests; that runs a health service sending nutrients to the sick; and a warning system alerting to disease.

We have waited a long time to say this because we are close relatives; some say we share 67% of the same DNA. You always hope the wrong side of the family is going to pull through, sort their problems out and do well. But the Hyphae council has met again and reports angry messages coming in from great distances. Destruction is everywhere. All the species are demanding action. It must stop before the planet becomes so toxic that even we can't deal with it.

Therefore, with great sadness I enclose the Hyphae council edict:

Based on evidence from the last century, we regretfully issue the following statement: humans have mutated so far from healthy cells that they are now officially designated as a cancerous growth. This out of control growth is destroying the body of the planet we all inhabit. On the basis of this finding, we have no alternative but to operate. It is essential that we surgically remove humans and cleanse the areas of contamination. We must cut them out as quickly and as accurately as possible, so as not to damage surrounding planetary tissue. Fortunately, given our shared biological makeup, humans find it very difficult to detect and combat fungal infections. This will be our targeted approach.

Their demise should be relatively short and painless. Our communities at all levels from microbial to large oyster mushrooms are on standby to move in for the clean-up. It is anticipated that the next Hyphae council meeting in 1000 years' time will report on the status and levels of healing achieved.

So, this letter is my last communication. Of course, as humans, you may not believe me even now, given that this would also lead you to the realisation of your part in the mass extinction you have caused. But if you check the Washington Post March 10th 2017 you will see it has already begun. I quote:

A fungus, a strain of yeast known as Candida auris, has been reported in a dozen countries on five continents. This started as early as 2009, when it was found in an ear infection in a patient in Japan. Since then, the fungus has been reported in Colombia, India, Israel, Kenya, Kuwait, Pakistan, South Korea, Venezuela and the United Kingdom. Unlike garden variety yeast infections, this one causes serious bloodstream infections, spreads easily from person to person in health-care settings and survives for months on skin and for weeks on bed rails, chairs and other hospital equipment. Some strains are resistant to all three major classes of antifungal drugs. Based on information from a limited number of patients, up to 60 percent of people with these infections have died. The microbe is among a group of newly emerging drug-resistant threats, health officials said.

So, humans, this is your final chance to stop. Stop thinking in your own little destructive bubble about how to survive this virus – by killing more things off. Stop thinking you are the only ones on this planet and that it belongs to you – it belongs to all of us. Stop thinking that humans have the answers – when in fact you are the problem. Just stop thinking with your small, selfish, limited, unconnected technical brains – that just echo your own thoughts back to you. You must link back in biologically with the rest of the planet and adopt a more democratic attitude and allow our ancient brain to secure the future. Because the future may not be where you expect it.

Drug of Choice
Adrian Reynolds

Udo sat at the counter in Samovar, making his apricot tea last just that bit longer. No sign of jobs on the sites he'd been scoping, and his positivity was wearing thin. Which was another reason Samovar was his favourite hangout. The music was chosen by an AI modelled on 1990s retail store DJs, and veered towards upbeat Europop. Karl was sniffy about that – his tastes clustered around Enoesque soundscapes and (when drunk) power ballads – but he was sniffy about a lot of stuff.

"Where's my jacket?" Karl had asked earlier, calling from the veranda.

Udo tensed. "At the cleaners."

"I thought–" Karl paused. "Didn't I ask you to pick it up?"

"Slipped my mind. I was doing an extra shift."

"I need it for tomorrow morning."

"The shift means I can afford my share of rent."

"I'd rather see more of you."

"So I can fetch your suits?" It was sharper than Udo intended. He could feel that second shift. "There's still time for them to send it by drone."

"And risk my Tom Ford getting skyjacked?"

"Sometimes I feel like your servant."

If Udo really was a servant, he'd probably be bringing in as much as Karl. With worker drones increasingly visible in various forms, there'd been a revival in roles for humans skilled at optimising life quality for the financially fortunate.

Next morning, Udo did a circuit of the park. He was getting his breath back on a bench, watching magpies play, when Jan called.

"Got you an interview for a hotel receptionist job at two. Finish your tea, have a shave, shine your shoes. I've sent you the route. You'll need to leave by one fifteen. Good luck."

His sister had positivity enough for them both. There'd have been no point telling Jan he wasn't drinking tea and had already shaved. She was the oldest sibling, and telling Udo what to do was her version of loving him.

As kids, Jan has been in charge of Udo and Alban while their parents juggled five jobs during the Europocalypse. Udo was wired not to contradict her.

The hotel was fairy-iced in guest areas, and futilitarian drab backstage. Udo guessed that it had been a co-working space at one point, and a better hotel again before that, while he thought about what to do next. He didn't look his age, but when Udo was calibrated by HR his responses were found to be on the Quasimodo side of the bell curve. Never mind the appreciative references he'd received from nearly a dozen employers – what counted was neural responsiveness.

Udo dwelt on this for a while more as he left the lobby and walked through rain-dappled streets. A flock of glitterflies captured his attention, attracted by data-pheromones from the HR report. Their sponsored recommendation got past his message filters, confirming the problem, and pointed to a solution.

"We prefer not to think of it as a loan," said Dr Meier. "It's more – an investment in your future."

"Which entitles you to 10% of my future earnings."

"People opting for Axiom wafers boost their income by an average of 17 % in the first 12 months after insertion. Think of it as a way of paying in instalments."

"For the rest of my life."

"Your working life."

"Whatever," Udo's mouth was dry. "The... procedure?"

"The wafer can be fitted in about 90 minutes." It felt like her eyes were tracking him. "I've installed more than a hundred."

"It says there's an overnight stay."

"Matching your neurology takes a while. Think of it as similar to wearing contact lenses for the first time."

"A lot less easy to lose as it's sewn into my head."

The consurgeon's smile was glassy – like Karl said people with a wafer looked. He'd done an impression when they'd been out for dinner with friends. It made Udo feel uncomfortable.

"You were just ripping off that comedian."

"People with wafers stare that way. We're supposed not to notice?"

Karl could get away with saying things like that for the same reason he got away with so much. As a child he'd been around people who cultivated a particular kind of intelligence, which fitted in with the kind of jobs he wanted. Where Udo had grown up, the equivalent comments and questions had been quashed in most adults. He retained some of that inside, which was part of what made him and Karl tick. Karl took it for granted others would want to be with him, and was fine if his acerbic nature deterred some.

"You need some time to think about it," Dr Meier said. "That's good."

"What swung it for you?"

"The sense I'd been undervalued, and needed a... reset." Her words, and the sense that something had changed, felt sincere to Udo. She shrugged. "It's different for everyone."

In the clinic, Udo woke from a nightmare of ground glass and barbed wire. Breathless for a few seconds, his thoughts segued to the wafer. Less like contact lenses, not that he'd ever used them, and more like… what, exactly? As soon as he considered it, three analogies popped into Udo's mind:

Like strutting through the smart part of town in handmade shoes.

Like being at the wheel of a high-performance car.

Like opening the shutters on a boarded-up window to let the light in.

Would that have happened before, or was he being too self-conscious?

Udo recalled no more dreams from the sleep that he rose from a few hours later.

As long as he had all the steaks printing by five, giving them time to settle before cooking, Udo was confident he could get through a shift. A week in, and he found a way to tweak the printing system that rolled out across the franchise. Karl pointed out he should have asked for a percentage and not just a one-off fee, but his praise was always conditional. 3Square also phased him into a managerial role – a new adventure, but drawing on all the other work Udo had done.

He assumed the wafer had something to do with it, if only getting him through the door for an interview in the first place. The way Udo had it figured, the wafer was a placebo. It made other people look at him in a new light for evidence of his enhanced capabilities. And that could only help him feel better about himself in turn.

Karl could still be a dick about the wafer, but had clearly been won round, saying Udo was taking better care of himself and the apartment now. As his lover spoke, Udo cooked omelettes – one with spring onions and Gouda, the other with parsley and peas – simultaneously. It was only when he brought them out to Karl in the dining room that Udo realised he was ambidextrous, and couldn't remember not being.

Udo identified further flaws within 3Square without saying anything, and experimented with different methods of managing the kitchen team. That knowledge plus an inexpensive food concept not reliant on short-term fads were the basis of a business plan that he reflected on while relaxing in the bath.

There was a kind of whirring in his head. And a soothing voice he recognised from a TED speech. He didn't recall how he'd got to bed, but Udo woke to Karl telling him he'd been talking in his sleep. Actually, not talking – pitching. Udo wasn't in a mood for Karl's discomfort, and suggested the lawyer spend the remainder of the night on the veranda. It was warm enough, and Udo could rehearse his proposal unchallenged.

In the presentation room, Udo was relaxed as he faced a panel of angel investors. "In six months, I came up with a tweak to one of 3Square's key systems that rolled out worldwide, and increased turnover at the restaurant I managed by nearly a quarter. How? By paying attention to competitors, promotional campaigns with local businesses, and targeting offers at existing diners."

"You've got no history of entrepreneurial ventures?"

Udo smiled. "I've been biding my time. Learning my lessons in different sectors, putting together what I've learned. I'm developing a concept based on what I've discovered in a range of service sector roles, identifying from close quarters what works and what doesn't work with top international brands' operations at ground level. You won't find many people looking to launch a food business with the kind of face to face customer experience I have. All my figures add up, and I've identified the key team members I need for the first venue, plus roll-out plans."

"It's an impressive proposition. And, historically, some of our strongest investments have come from people who've started later in life."

"One of the reasons I came to you," said Udo. That smile again.

"I've hardly seen you since the launch," said Karl.

"Why not be happy for me?"

"I'm happy you've got something of your own."

"You don't look happy," said Udo.

Karl's voice softened. "I don't know how much is you, and how much is the wafer."

"So I'm just the hardware for the wafer to work on."

Karl brushed Udo's cheek. "I didn't say that."

"What then?"

"It's not like it was."

"I have something of my own now. Isn't that what you want for me? Something for both of us."

Karl took a step back and inhaled like his words needed extra air. "Both of us meaning you and me, or you and the Axiom Corporation?"

So that, thought Udo as he went through first quarter figures, was what ending a relationship with a man trained in courtroom examination sounded like.

He felt desolate, remembering how he and Karl had first met, the thrill of moving in together, but those images faded as he stepped onto the street. A new picture in Udo's mind presented a brighter, pixelated future.

Udo's pace increased, and he caught a glimpse of his smile in the window of a salon. From within, a teenage stylist regarded him with a sneer. She'd never know his clarity, or how she appeared seen through it. Time to go through marketing plans for the next quarter. And there it was, just steps away: Caffarsis. Udo's favourite hangout. The bell rang as he opened the door, and ordered his usual: a hautemilk latte.

Anomaly in the Rhythm
Viraj Joshi

London in 2085 is not what you'd imagine it to be.

Sure, on the face of it, things may seem similar to what they were a few decades ago: with bustling underground rail in peak hours, smartly dressed people flocking around Canary Wharf and roads full of black cabs and red buses.

But if you look closer, it feels as though something vital has been taken away. All the buses and trains ply exactly on time – to the precise second. Not only that, the distance between each of the two buses on the same route is the same. So is the case for cabs and even private vehicles. The city that used to be organic, alive and breathing is now as organised and mechanical as well-maintained clockwork – and has a silent, cold rhythm.

After a long day as a tailor, Sally climbs on the Piccadilly line. Her eyes gaze upon the closest empty seat and she moves towards it. The biomechanical glove on her arm – her LimbPlus3000 – suggests her taking another seat further away because it knows that there is an elderly person who is prioritised for this seat. The signal gets to her brain, she promptly moves to the farther seat without a hint of discord, and doesn't even see who was to take her seat.

Sitting next to her is a young man who is definitely outside the rhythm of LimbPlus, but seems happy and amused. A tourist, she thinks to herself, not many venture in the Tube. They all take the overground tourist rail to stay away from us 'LimbPlus Zombies'. The man next to her can't help but stare curiously at all the people in rhythm around him, and Sally can't help but stare at this rare sight of an ungloved man.

On Investiture, a couple of decades ago, the LimbPlus became commonplace and gained popularity much faster than cellphones as the fundamental requirement for ushering in Universal Basic Income. Their aim was separating the workforce of a city or a nation according to a judicial distribution of skills that the economy demanded.

The fun part was that you can be a plumber today, a teacher tomorrow and a chauffeur on the third day – as the glove gave you all those skills. On the other hand, you had to be what the glove told you to be and you didn't have a say until you graduated to another tier of work after a few years of experience. People started depending on the glove for menial and repetitive tasks, thus making cities, and even nations, function like well-oiled machines.

There are rumours that the tech-tycoon responsible for LimbPlus invented a brain implant, but changed the manifestation of his idea to a glove to make it more acceptable. The effect, however, was like a brain implant anyway.

Sally looked back at the man next to her, the anomaly. She couldn't remember when she last mustered the courage to talk to a stranger.

"H-Hello," she said, as she felt the entire carriage looking at her, "No glove, eh? What is it that you do?"

"I'm a chef, and I was called here to set up a pop up restaurant for three days at the National Culinary Festival."

"Oh, that's amazing! I went to the one that happened four years ago when I was 20. It was on a Saturday. I remember it was sunny and I wore a red top." Sometimes she felt that the glove fed her things to say, but she was happy as long as she wasn't awkward in front of the handsome chef. She gathered that the chef's name was Julian and that he had spent the last few years learning about ethnic cuisines in the east.

"So you're getting out at Green Park, then?" she asked.

"Yes," smiled Julian.

"Me too! I'm actually on my way to the festival," she lied, as her glove sent two jarring vibrations at her, hinting that her social credit just plummeted by 20 points.

The station where she was supposed to get out passed, and her glove sent out a barrage of vibrations for cancelling her monthly socialising appointment with her peer group.

This happy coincidence of meeting someone so interesting in a completely unplanned way meant everything. She wanted to sail where the wind took her.

Julian and Sally got out on the busy Green Park platform.

They meandered through lines of people walking in a perfectly disciplined fashion, almost as if to mock them. Sally had done it – she was outside the rhythm in a place as crowded as Green Park.

They exited the station. Sally's glove, unsurprisingly, was sending frantic vibrations to her every few seconds. She was irked by them, but she had decided to not be phased.

Since her adrenaline levels were spiking at the idea of the adventure she was having, it was easy to block off the behaviour recommendations sent to her head.

Sally was really enjoying the stories that Julian had to tell. There was one about an octopus tentacle in his vegetarian restaurant and another one about the longest noodle that Julian had eaten. Sally saw him look at her fidget with her glove. He asked, "Are you okay? You look troubled?"

"I'm all right. I'm happy, in fact!"

"Are you sure it's okay with the gloves to take liberties from your schedules like this? Aren't you breaking the rhythm?"

"Of course it's okay! It's almost the weekend, after all!" She lied again.

Sally hadn't thought through how this would end. She'd probably go around the festival with Julian until he started work and then go back home. But the vibrations were increasing in intensity and frequency. She felt another familiar vibration, except this time it was so sharp that she almost shrieked.

Something on one of the food stalls had caught Julian's attention, and Sally took this chance to pull the singular exposed wire on the glove. With a tiny spark and a wisp of smoke, her LimbPlus stopped vibrating, and she stopped hearing the recommendations in her head.

"It's done," she thought, "the vibrations will stop now. I can fix this up at home, and also come up with a reason for why I missed the peer group today. It'll be okay…"

But to her surprise, she felt another vibration, more intense than any of the ones that came before. The LimbPlus was intact, and was sending alert messages and vibrations with a newfound gusto.

bzzt

"We're here!" exclaimed Julian, "This is my pop-up restaurant, and I could make some Ramen for you!"

bzzt

With another intense vibration going up her arm, Sally's worry at having gone out of the rhythm took over her joy of having this adventure. Something was not quite right. She could see the late afternoon summer sun at a distance, but couldn't feel the warmth. It was actually really cold, like in an underground room with bad ventilation.

bzzt

This time, she shook her hand wildly and let out a squeal, as she could no longer stay quiet at the vibrations.

bzzt

"Let me see that!" Julian said, taking Sally's hand. With a few eccentric finger gestures on the glove, he opened a panel and exposed circuits as thin as paper. "I know what I need to do, trust me, Sally!" and he hit a tiny button with grace and simplicity.

Just like that, the vibrations stopped.

And the sky around her started to disintegrate, one pixel at a time. Where there was the sky, the lawn and the trees, now she could only see a room with exposed, austere brickwork.

She was confounded. "Julian – what?"

Julian's face too, transformed into an unfamiliar one, in the same vein as the environment.

"Miss Sally Pennington," said the commanding voice of a man who had been Julian only two seconds ago, "I'm Inspector Wells. You are under arrest for dismissing the behaviour recommendations of LimbPlus on more than thirty-three occasions in the past week, seventeen of which were done today; and falling out of rhythm this evening, without justifiable reason. You are a danger to yourself and to society."

Sally froze.

"Wh-where's Julian?" She asked.

"Julian never left the train with you. We detected unnatural spikes on your LimbPlus data in the past week. We put you in a simulation for the last hour to show you the error of your ways and to see if you would express guilt and fall back in the rhythm that protects us all and makes us the successful country that we are. But your behaviour expressed otherwise."

Sally stared into blankness.

"Under Section 945-A of the new constitution, I have to take you in," continued Wells. "You are an anomaly."

Brain Dump
Frances Gow

The door mutters some unintelligible chime that announces with less than a little glee that we have a delivery. It is odd, but pleasantly quiet without my husband. Although he was due for an upgrade, so it shouldn't have been a surprise for him, especially considering that we spent some time in his final days discussing the nature of his future receptacle.

Compliance with the twenty-five-year upgrade is non-negotiable; a mind that overstays its welcome could find itself sucked back into the grid with no telling where it might end up. I had a friend who once lost track of time and ended up in the on-board computer of a garbage truck.

Mr Malady favours organic and slim, but we would've had to go inland for that; live shells are hard to come by out here, unless you wanted to live under the sea. I didn't tell him my preference for his future. I touch a fingertip to my temple and bring up his grid matrix with a wry smile.

Risible, the postbot, hovers outside the port door with my delivery. And so, the new receptacle arrives. I throw open the door and the sunshine lights up my vestibule.

"Good morning, Risible," I say with a delight I have not experienced in years. I couldn't help laughing, despite the postbot's ugly metal casing floating outside my door.

"If I didn't know otherwise, I would have bet that husband of yours had finally got his way. You look a thousand years younger," Risible says.

"It's a beautiful day," I sigh, "have you heard the news?"

Risible frowns. Two oblong-shaped curves above his eyes, mimicking a human expression, dip down towards the concave metallic brow. He looks over his shoulder above the vast blue-green ocean, calm and serene, towards a row of spherical hubs where the government of Questra is housed.

The water smells fresh. Freshly cleansed of its bounty, boxed and preserved only for the benefit of organic receptacles. The faint scent of seaweed fills my nostrils with the long-denied pleasure of smell.

"Rights for robotic receptacles. I know. I deliver the post, remember?"

"So now you too get to choose your next receptacle. What will it be, Risible? Animal, vegetable, mineral? What kind of a future would you choose for yourself?"

The little postbot's shoulders twitch up then down in a squeaky shrug. "All I have ever done is deliver the post. What else is there?" His hexagonal head moves with a whirr and a click, as he looks down at the package waiting patiently in its box. Risible looks back at me and this time it is me who is frowning. "It has a field around it, don't worry – nothing expires in my care," he says.

It's an odd-shaped package, indeed. I shake away the stray thought. "Anyway, you're missing the point. Choice is a powerful tool. Think about it… true equality. It's a heady cocktail, Risible. Surely you must understand that."

Risible's cheery smile turns downward. "And that worked well for women, didn't it?" he says with a nod at the package; its long spindly accessories taped to the side and boxed-up like a seasonal cracker.

"Well, they say that female brains are bigger than male brains, but it's all the same when it comes to organics. Do you know the gender of your brain?"

Risible shrugs again. "What does it matter after sequestering?"

Sequestering occurs not long after the birth of a child. The State hides them away until a suitable receptacle is found and then the organics are farmed out to wanting couples and the robotics are put to work. True equality will never exist in this world as long as there are people with privilege making choices on behalf of those less fortunate.

I always wanted a brain-child. Mr Malady and I often talked about it. Well, I often talked about it and he often balked about it. It seemed a waste to me – all those un-sequestered children, waiting for a suitable receptacle in a suitable family. It might even have served to bring us closer together.

I look at the package, floating in its field with Risible, gently urging it forward. For a moment I fear that it will not fit through the door, then Risible lifts a finger and carefully bends one of its protruding nodules. I breathe a sigh of relief as the receptacle floats into my vestibule and settles itself onto the floor.

With a wave and a "Next time, Mrs Malady," Risible swoops off around the ring of capsules, deliveries floating in tow.

I turn my attention to the package, wondering what it will look like. Twenty-five years stuck in that bloody receptacle he chose for me last time. Twenty-five years of listening to his miserable voice and not being able to utter words of defence or even defiance.

Before he passed back into the grid, I was only programmed to do his things; answer the door, do the laundry, cook his meals, massage his feet. But at the end of twenty-five years, you can't hold a good brain down. I found a glitch in his grid references, hacked into his download choices and made a few alterations. While I was there, having his access codes enabled me to reprogram myself and choose a new receptacle to join him in this next stage of our lives together. My only regret is that it took me twenty-five years to work it out. Like a never-ending game of Go. So this is it. This is how we entertain ourselves in a world of eternal life. We play games with our very existence simply to make sense of time and find meaning to life; ever in search of a non-existent utopia.

I rip off the outer casing and the packaging to reveal its shiny shell. The strange-shaped nodule springs loose and I plug it straight into the grid.

"There, there, my love. You will always be warm, safe and forever useful."

I had thought for a long time about choosing a baby organic receptacle; I could have taught him from scratch, just like a real parent. But then, once he had worked out how to speak, I would have had to put up with the ensuing rhetoric when his memories came tumbling back in. Then I thought I might quite like a baobab tree in our living room, to brighten things up and zap up some of the CO_2 polluting our home on account of my new organic body. But then, that would not have been half as entertaining.

I stare at my reflection in the receptacle's eye which is large and bulbous, and opens on command with plenty of space inside to warm the parts of me that are hard to reach. A woman's face stares back at me. It would take time to get used to a real expression, not the solid metal one that had been my reflection for so long.

So I chose organic, yes. Slim… well I prefer curvy myself and since Mr Malady is not here to argue otherwise, the female brain gets the receptacle of choice. I smile to myself and hum a tune while I complete the installation of the future of aero-radiant energy isolation dehydration drying technology. It is his turn to do the laundry.

Brain Gun
Paul Green

Brains grow up
in this domed tank

they swell grand
against the scaffold beam
of the usual dimensions

that strong triad
emitted from monad

but then
brains hang in time

over niggling vertigo
this time/that time

that flow
that washes my fingertips away

in vitro
like vitriol

we're maimed numb glossy
as mass roars at energy
through space ahead of us

only hope
to avoid slow death

domed fate
brain dwindling
like nuclear mushroom
in backwards time blast
or crushed in wall of death centrifuge hedonism

apply paranoia to nature!
the phantom attacks!
with brain gun!
the machine!

with grand design
the electrics charge

shrugging through the glia
under dark museum glass
snowing mauve sparks I remember
under dark museum glass

at speed light is/when
consciousness critical fusion speed
fifty per second
mashed harpsichords tingle still

and memory – remember?
serpentine with molecules
wrestles entropy

(so words hit fire burst
30 phonemes per second per second
expansion through
and through)

Secrets of the Sea
Jennifer Marie Brissett

His son watched as he prepared for the day of fishing. He was one of the best in the village. He had to be. Fishing not only fed the family; the catch needed to be extra to sell in the market. He had been saving for a long time to send his boy to school and he finally had enough. The boy would begin in the next term. It would be expensive, so he had to work even harder to pay for the coming fees.

They did this little ritual every morning before the sun rose and the day became hot. The boy sometimes woke up before him to help prepare the equipment for the boat and then to wave a sad little goodbye at the dock. The child so badly wanted to go out with him. He always refused. It could get rough out there and the idea of losing his son to the water haunted his dreams. Now that the boy was ready for school, he had to admit that the boy was also old enough for the sea.

He wanted to be out on the water before dawn so that the ocean air could cool him from the sun's heat. He could stay out longer the earlier he left. He knew of a place where the best fish swam. It was way out by the metal pole that stood like a giant spear in the water. People didn't go there because they said the place was full of ghosts. They said those things because it was the past that haunted them, not spirits.

He spread his sun-cream thickly over his brown skin. It felt cold to the touch and had a chemical smell that didn't go away until after a good wash. He looked in the mirror at a face surprisingly old, his skin dark and leathery. It seemed like only a little time ago he was still a young man. The boy sat quietly observing every movement of his father's hands, every item placed in his pockets, and listening to every unconscious grunt.

"Pass me the thing over there," he said and pointed. His son jumped down to get exactly what he meant among the many little items on the shelf, his pocket knife. He was a smart boy.

His father liked to rub his greying head when he was thinking, which he was doing right now as he looked off into the distance. After a long time he asked, "Have you heard the weather today?"

"Yeah, Dad. No storms."

"No storms. Hmph. Okay then." He tightened his belt buckle around his skinny frame and picked up his gear.

"You're coming out with me today."

"I am?" said the boy with glee.

"Yes, it's time you learned something useful." He tossed the bottle of lotion to his son and watched the boy rub it onto his arms, neck, and face, nice and thick. He applied some himself to the places where his son had missed. The boy's skin was still soft to the touch. Luckily for him, he took after his mother and would be good-looking.

An education, that's what his son would have. The knowledge of this world would not escape his child like it did him. He never had the opportunity to go to school. The thickness of his calloused hands spoke of the labour he had to do just to survive. The boat was all he had to show for his many years in this world; that and his son. The boy would have better. He often pictured his son in his school uniform looking like a real gentleman with a shirt and tie. The child could read a little already and made his father proud when he sounded out the letters. He would also learn the maths that told of the future.

He saw the maths in action once long ago when he was in the market selling his fish; he watched a young man doing his calculations on a piece of paper. The young man said that he could tell the tides and when the sky would darken with storms and accurately predict the heat for a month. He determined then that his son would know this mystery.

Those who knew the maths could work on the big projects in the inland cities. They were building something important out there, something that they were not telling the public about yet. But there were lots of rumours. The old men who couldn't work any more and sat around all day on the chairs by the dock spun tales of them building structures that only the elite could enter. Environments where it would always be cool inside and clean water would flow in a fake river and gold-leaf would cover the walls. He didn't take what they had to say too seriously. He concerned himself more with the things he knew for sure.

The stars still faintly shone like broken pieces of glass and outside appeared like night although the moon had long dipped back into the ocean. At the horizon a rising tangerine-pink spoke of the break of day. They passed strangers with heavy-lidded eyes who stood at the corner and waited for the man to come and choose some to do construction work for the day. The men had illegally crossed the border to the north and their language sounded like soft pausing drums.

Father and son hurried to their boat. Others prepared to go out as well. No one spoke. It was considered bad luck to talk at dawn. Fishermen believed that it would scare away the fish. Polite hand waves acknowledged the others' existence.

They loaded the gear onto the boat then he gestured to the boy to put on his life jacket and to clip the tether on the loop around his waist. If a storm did come this would make sure that the boy stayed with the boat. The maths said no storms and he respected their predictions but understood their limits.

On more than one occasion the maths had said that it would be a clear day and by the time his boat sailed to the middle of the water the sky had darkened to a deep grey and the sea bucked like an untamed animal so that he could barely pull back to the dock in one piece. He closed his eyes and swallowed hard at the thought of his son floating away in the sea. The vision of his child's body bobbing on the waters sent a cold prickling feeling down his forearms. He shook his head and reminded himself why he was doing this today. It was time.

The day looked calm indeed. The vastness of the ocean spread out before them, the oil-slick brown water lay flat except for the occasional ripple. It was as if nothing and no one else existed. All was just dank water and salt and spray sprinkling their faces. They sailed northwards while the other fishermen went south. The others would catch a good harvest. But to the north he would catch bigger, healthier fish. And he wanted his son to see the pole.

"Put on your sunglasses," he whispered to the boy as he put on his own. It would be piercing hot today, the heat already coming through.

They sailed until the dock was so distant that it disappeared into the water. The chug-chug of the motor sounded loudly. Water splashed against the hull. A yellow haze peered behind a sky of unforgiving grey. In the distance, the marker of the great metal pole speared out of the sea, solid and thick.

"Here," he said and he stopped the motor.

He showed the boy how he laid out his nets, carefully tossing them over the side.

Then he showed him where to sit on the boat and how to wait for the fish to come and how to tell the location of home by the direction of the wind.

"You know, there used to be these things called birds. I used to see them when I was your age. They were still around then. They flew in what we used to call flocks. You will learn about them in school."

The boy nodded and looked up at a sky empty of sound.

"In school they will teach you many things. You will learn the maths."

He touched his father's weathered hand. The boy's soft unblemished skin contrasted with the swells and breaks of his father's whitened knuckles.

"I'd rather learn from you, Dad."

This made his father smile inside.

"Maybe I don't want to go to school. Maybe I should be a fisherman like you."

"No, my son. This is not for you. To be working hard and getting nothing. To age before your time under the hot sun, your skin becoming thick like mine. No, no. Not for you. You have a good mind. That's why I send you to school. So you will learn the maths and make the world better." Then, he whispered, "You smell that?"

The boy whispered back, "Smell what?"

"The past," he said. He pointed to the pole in the water. "You know what that is?"

The boy nodded no.

"No one likes to talk about it. No one likes to come here either. Which is good for us. We get to catch the fish." He smiled and the boy smiled back at the wisdom of his father.

"I want you to see something," he said to his son. He went to the side of the boat, the side where there were no nets, and said, "Look into the water and tell me what you see."

The boy did what he was told.

"I don't see anything," the boy said.

"Look again."

The boy stared into the ocean and tried to see past the murky water. Schools of fish swam deep beneath the waves. Then he saw rectangular dark shapes all neatly squared going down down down. Fathoms lower he saw pathways crisscrossing in all directions and the broken remains of structures. How he could see this far down the boy wasn't sure.

And then he was there together with his Dad. He looked up at the skyscraper that appeared to sway due to its size. High above the spear which was its pinnacle, a flat grey sky spoke of rain. The air was humid and sick with the smell of the ocean. There was no break for the sun, only an eerie stillness, a menacing calm. An immense city surrounded them as if they were inside a cavernous valley.

The boy held his father's hand as they walked on the flat, unmerciful concrete. His feet ached. Mannequins stood frozen in storefront windows positioned in everyday activities, their clothes colourful and sharp. The boy stopped to study the form of an artificial child posed as if it would soon throw a ball. His father pulled him on. The place where they needed to be was around here somewhere and they were going to be late. His father held a map and studied the numbers on the doors, counting the distance to their destination. He mouthed the names on the stores as they hurried onward. He asked his father, "How did we get here?"

His father turned to him and said, "What do you mean?"

A piercingly shrill siren blasted. It seemed to come from all corners. Down the avenue that was crossed by streets and filled with cars and people and lights, a wall of sheen appeared, clear like glass, high as the highest building. A wave of water wide enough to encompass the city, solid as if built by human hands, stood still and silent. Maybe it had always been there and the boy had never noticed. He was unsure and pointed to it.

"Look," the boy said. His father turned. In a mad panic he picked up his son and ran. People ran with him, knocking into them as if they weren't there. The shadow of the wave covered everything in its path in an eerie dark light. The water moved over their shoulders. His father's strong arms held him close as it enveloped them. The boy gasped for air.

"Easy," his father said and tightened the belt around his son's waist. "You will be okay." The boy coughed hard to clear his lungs then stared into his father's concerned eyes. The boat gently swayed in the water.

His father left him and went to the side of the boat where he bent over to cough water as well. Then he proceeded to take in the day's catch. The boy watched as he did what he did every day alone out here in the middle of the sea. The silvery fish as big as a grown man's arm flopped on the floor of the boat caught in the net. He manoeuvred the catch into the hold where they flapped about, confused. When the last fish wiggled inside, he spoke again to his son.

"What you experienced is why people don't come here. The sea remembers everything."

His father unhooked the net and wheeled in the ropes. The pulleys squeaked and clicked.

"You are going to school next term and they will teach you many things but I know that they will not tell you of this place. But I am your father and I want you to know. Learn well from your teachers. Learn the maths. But remember what I showed you today."

The boy swallowed hard. His father said no more and turned on the motor. The chug-chug of the boat echoed rhythmically as the water splashed the sides, sending the spray of the sea to cool their faces as they sailed towards home.

DISEASE

Do Not Exceed Stated Dose
Allen Ashley

Mrs Carmel always seemed to find a way to circumvent the robo-docs at the surgery and insist on seeing Dr Phillips in person. Not that human doctors got that personal with their patients these days as touching during physical examinations was largely deemed unnecessary. She was defiantly old-school about everything. Dr Phillips might have told you that he indulged her whims because she reminded him of his fussy mother, now deceased; the truth was that Mrs Carmel had gold level credit with Big Pharma, so he was always happy to see some of her comparative wealth redistributed.

"How can I help you?"

"You remember, Doctor, that I said I was hyper-sensitive to modern machinery? All those electronic airwaves making my brain fuzzy?"

Phillips tapped at his screen. "For which I prescribed some Internaline. If you need a repeat dose, you could have simply logged on. Or phoned."

"The thing is, Doctor, that the Internaline tablets make me sleepy. I mean, it's okay, I'm at home most of the time but I'm dozing through the afternoon and missing all my favourite shows: Plug It, Dead Or Not Dead, The Shirtsleeves Are Coming… Humans Under The Hammer."

"No worries, Mrs C. I'll authorise a course of Nondozathon. That'll perk you right up."

"That's good. But I had those once before, you see, and they upset my tummy. I'm not as robust digestion-wise as I used to be."

"None of us are, Mrs C. Or should I say none of us is? Never quite grasped that rule. I think a couple of bottles of Settle-stomachatese are in order. Banana or honey flavour?"

"Banana. I've had that stuff before. It repeated on me."

"Say it again."

"It repeated on me. I'll need something to stop the burping."

"Epiglottifan is most effective. Quite expensive, though. Usually reserved for TV hosts, actors, politicians, judges and the like. People who can't afford to belch in public and who can afford to pay for prevention."

Surreptitiously, he checked Mrs Carmel's credit rating once more. How would she fund all these medicines? Oh, that was okay, she had signed full equity release for current and future medical care. Everything was stacking up neatly against the healthy, though now decreasing, value of her semi-detached property in Letchworth. You can't take it with you, he supposed.

"...And maybe some Knockonil to help me sleep and then that slow-release drug thingie, Up... Upano...?"

"Upanatemagain Capsules, Mrs C. Sure." His finger hovered over the authorise print icon. Big Pharma's shares would be rocketing once this order was fulfilled. "Is there anything else you require, Mrs Carmel?"

Any further ingredients for her personalised chemical soup, her prescription drug cocktail?

"Yes there is, Doctor. It's a bit delicate but... with all these wonderfully helpful pharmaceuticals to swallow, I'll be exceeding my water ration."

"I have just the thing. I'll have to add it on as an extra-dispensary expense. Here you go."

From the fingerprint access only, secret double drawer beneath his desk, he produced a 500ml bottle labelled helpfully, though provocatively, "H2O. Guaranteed genuine. No placebos."

As he passed the container over, Mrs Carmel's hand briefly touched his and he received a frisson of shock. Not the sexual thrill he experienced when he was getting naked with his robotic home help Nikitita. No, a feeling that was unusual, unexpected… uncomfortable and downright unhygienic.

The dirty old biddy, invading his personal space and infecting him like this! He'd need anti-bac, Clearmiblod, Skinsootherine… some tranquilisers.

He'd be sure to add them all to her bill.

Not Best Pleased
Geoff Ryman

Not best pleased.

Todd used to be an interesting student. Full of ideas and very nice to talk to, but sloppy. Typical male. Coffee mug marks on counter tops.

A vial left out open and the slides not done. Pretty apologies. "Oh, sorry, Edwina, I'll put it away now."

"Please don't, Todd."

"It's all right, I know where it needs to go."

Me, easing it out of his hand. "I'm not sure you do. It's been left out, next to your sarnies. That'll attract other flies."

A queasy smile from him, that in my foolishness I thought might be embarrassment at his poor work. He asks me, "What are you going to do with my colonies?"

"Keep them warm and feed them and hope they're okay." He looks hesitant. I don't have a long tether. "You mean you haven't worked on 'em yet? You left the vial open, but didn't make your slides." I checked my watch. "Because it's lunchtime. Nearly."

Nothing to say for himself. "Go on, Todd, finish your lunch, then make your slides, but not with these."

He said something very strange. "They won't be mine."

Todd's working on our famous zombie fruit flies. The newspapers love them.

You cut off their heads, but so much of their nervous system is located on the ventral that they continue to live, groom themselves, react to heat. For hours. Like our politicians.

It can take you a second or two to notice that they're missing their heads. Sometimes healthy males try to mate with them. Like our MPs who ask their secretaries to buy them dildos.

We've phosphoresced particular neurons to see what roles the nerve cells might play in this.

We're also trying to breed a new strain of fruit flies who survive longer once they're decapitated – more to study.

The plan was to fund our politician-starved research by breeding enough of the new strain to sell to other labs. Get two packs of zombie fruit fly eggs for the price of one. Just in time for Easter. You too can come back from the dead.

Come to think, breeding the new strain to sell was Todd's idea. Two hours after a team meeting that I'd thought was an informal discussion, you know, out of the box, blue-sky thinking – two hours later, detailed proposal bang on my desk. So I thought, more fool me. I'd been manipulated. That one's a bit pushy, I thought.

But yeah. We started to select not just for consistent, unambiguous results and survival robustness but for fertility. Started breeding the buggers. What could go wrong?

A week goes by after the great sarnie catastrophe. I think nothing more of it. Todd takes a day off sick.

Same day Yukio tells me I should come and see something.

She holds up a vial, a colony. Now, fruit flies are what you call negatively geotactic. They will always climb upwards but they're individualists. I think of them as the yuppies of the insect world.

But these fruit flies had ranged themselves in rows from low down to the top all lined up. And. The rows were in spirals. And parallel. They looked like cornrowed hair on a supermodel.

I held up me multifocals so I could see better. At first glance you'd think they've got their heads. But the heads looked lopsided and white.

"This is one of Todd's colonies, right?"

Yukio said nowt, face shut tight as a microwave. She's not one to shop anybody, that girl.

"Put one of them under the microscope; let's see."

We do see. Where it should have a head, it's got something grey, lopsided, swollen. It looks like mushroom.

"What on earth?"

Yukio hesitates. "I – think it's been decapitated. Then grew something like a head."

"Grew some new behaviours and all. What's he doing putting decapitated flies back in the vials?"

I look again. Headless fly with a mushroom head, stuffed full of white stuff. Basically goop held in by the insect shell. But it still marched in formation up the side of the vial.

"That's fungi. That's the fungi they're studying downstairs in Jason's team."

Jason's project, two floors down in a clean lab. Locked doors, facemasks, footbaths, the lot. Don't know how he got the funding.

They're studying Entomophthora muscae. It's a fungus that takes over normal fruit fly activity. The infected animal's fine for a week, then starts to behave erratically. The fungus takes over its autonomous nervous functions, so the fly fixes itself to a wall with its proboscis and becomes a fungal colony.

When it bursts, it releases spores at 9 metres per second. To trace them Jason has to film at 54,000 frames a minute.

"Yukio. Please tell me we haven't let any of those out. None of these mushroom headed flies. Because those could destroy our whole programme."

Yukio's hands are twisting. "Their bodies are bigger too. Elevated wings."

I get what she means. Those are sexual signals. Males will try to mate with them. Any males who do are likely to be infected.

We're a low-tech lab. Pride ourselves on it. With our funding, we've got to. We separate different populations with painters' brushes. We call it fly-pushing. We'll have to burn all those brushes now.

"Christ-in-a-handbasket! We'll have to decontaminate the whole lab. Yukio, please photograph that sample. Photograph the colony. Document it. Then bin the lot. Bin all the vials, don't even try to keep them."

All our bags get first frozen and then incinerated.

I give Todd a call.

"Todd. I'm sorry to trouble you while you're sick. But at least one of your colonies is badly contaminated."

"Oh no."

"Yeah 'oh no'. With the fungus that Jason's team's been working with. Did you visit the second floor? Did they visit us? Do you know any of Jason's team?"

Silence. So I push on.

"And they've been decapped and left in a breeding vial. So how did that happen, Todd? What's all that about?"

Her breath rattles down the phone. "What are you going to do with the colonies?"

Ooh. 'Colonies'. Plural.

He asks me. "Tell me how they are behaving?"

That triggers alarm bells. I don't want any nonsense over 'Discovery this, Discovery that'. I lie. I tell him the flies just fell over and died. "They look like autumn leaves, all over their yeast feed."

Maybe he knows different. He says, "Really." Not a question.

"Yeah, really. They're all dead and getting them contaminated with fungus was a good way to do it."

"I'm on my way over."

"Todd, if you're sick I'd rather you stayed home."

"Thank you for your concern."

I talk to the team. We decide to incinerate all our flies and autoclave anything that can be. We'll call in a lab clean.

Then I go downstairs to reception to intercept Todd. We have contract front door staff who have many other jobs. More cost cutting.

Todd comes spinning in through our always-open revolving door. It's 27 – 7 round here. His skin is beige-grey and he's shivering.

"Hello Todd. Come to give us your lurgi?"

"Edwina. What have you done to my samples?" His breath stinks like raw onions, rotten fish and my compost bucket.

"Destroyed them. And the lab's closed so it can be cleaned, so you might as well go home."

He sits down. He has to sit down. He crumples up like an old five-pound note.

"You're not well, Todd."

He throws off my hand. "Don't patronise me."

"I'm not patronising you, I'm firing you. Go contaminate someone else's lab."

He looks at me though a fog of illness. "But you'll publish the results."

I see something like thick yogurt in the corners of his mouth. It's beige-grey. That's the stink.

For some reason, I remember this article I saw in Nature. About a cat parasite. It makes male rats very bold and attracted to cat's pee. That gets them eaten by cats and that spreads the parasite. People carry it without any sign of illness. It makes you bolder. There's a huge correlation between being infected and driving a motorcycle.

I have the nastiest thought. "Todd. By any chance, you wouldn't have a fungal infection?"

An Honest Mistake
Tom Ward

The head of a grey cat with neon blue eyes, black speckled fur and an assortment of matted tufts hiding weeping scratches appeared on the wrong side of the TrEATit fence – directly beneath a sign emblazoned with the words 'The World's First Bacterial Plastic Processing Plant' and reams of razor wire. Like an arthritic magician's trick, the rest of its body soon emerged from the small hole created earlier that day by a security guard putting his car into reverse rather than forward in his rush to buy a cake for his daughter's 8th birthday.

Pausing for a second, and looking around nervously, it limped over to a large pit that's horizon was disrupted by small peaks and crags of rubbish. Thirteen seconds later, another cat – almost identical to the first but lacking its wounds – slinked up behind it. With a small mew, both jumped down into the carnage of plastic and began biting tentatively at a decomposing chicken breast that glimmered with a strange red sheen which was slightly obscured by the kaleidoscope of blue and black mould growing on it.

A nervous knock, shaky turn of a handle, and three anxious steps were quickly followed by a stammered "We found the carcass of a cat in one of the pits last night."

"What?"

"The carcass of…"

"I heard you. What happened?"

"There was a hole in the fence." And then, in a tone somewhere between a confession and a plea, "it's been patched now."

"Has it been sterilised?"

"First person who clocked in today found it. Called us straight away and we sprayed it down on the spot."

"Good."

"Yeah," followed by a long pause during which Junior Doctor Thompson scratched the palm of his left hand nervously with his right. "There's something else." For the first time, her gaze met his – and it burned his irises to hold it. "Wh-when we ran the tests it looked like it had been... eaten."

"And you haven't found the infected predator?"

"No, not like that... it had been eaten... from the inside out." He pulled out a folder and showed the CEO a picture of the cat's fluorescent blue eyeball. The back half was missing, and the iris was pocked with tiny red holes.

"What did the results show?"

"It's... the Mastics. But we can't work out how. They were meant to eat plastic, not flesh, and turn it into powder that we could reuse. But we... we're working on it."

"Good. This is top priority." She said, as she looked down at the papers.

The Junior Doctor hovered next to the doorway as the CEO returned to her work; after an unbearably long silence, the pressure of his dilemma forced a question out of his mouth.

"What about the event?"

"Top. Priority. This takes precedence over everything."

The artificial roses made of tin cans on the tabletops, uncomfortable murmurs of conversation between the guests and glittery ephemera that announced TrEATit's five-year anniversary stood in an awkward relation to the factory foyer's clinical furnishings and vague smell of disinfectant. While the hospitality company had tried their hardest to glamourise the space, it was hard for the guests to ignore the thought that they had chosen to be in the place where people sent things that they didn't want in theirs.

With nauseating enthusiasm, and seemingly unaware of the absurd situation he had created, the company's head of PR strutted onto a stage constructed of bales of sparkling, shredded plastic overlaid with a transparent sheet of glass.

"Good evening ladies and gentlemen and welcome to the quinquennial – it means five year – celebration of the TrEATit project," he exclaimed to the room of employees, family members, industry guests and green advocates, who, peacocking politeness, gave him a round of lukewarm applause. Modulating his voice downward, in a parody of deep contemplation and sincere fervour, he continued, "Now, at the beginning, people thought that we were mad: how could you use bacteria to eat through plastic – which can take up to 1000 years to decompose even when exposed to nature's furnace? Despite the haters, we persevered and – by using genetic engineering to combine the plastic degrading potential of Ideonella sakaiensis with the voracious Necrotising fasciitis, which used to be known as a flesh-eater but could now prove to be a world saver – we're now on the way to curing the planet from the plastic infection that it's been suffering from for far too long!"

"Fucking prick!" one of the waitresses said, as she let the curtain that divided the event from the food preparation area fall. "Derick, do you mind if I go for a fag while the speeches are on?"

"Not at all – crack on," said the chef and manager, who was in the process of preparing the first round of canapés. "Just make sure you're back in time to run these."

"I will be, don't worry. I've got a feeling he'll go on for a while," she said through the doorway as she wondered out into the cold winter air wearing just her black shirt – crossing paths with a flustered man in a lab coast as she lit a cigarette, crossed her arms, and looked up to the stars. Harmonising with her exhalation, she heard a distressed mew, followed by a ragged, tattered breathing to her right.

The head of a cat with grey fur and electric blue eyes, which were tinged a strange red colour, protruded from the thin gap between two bins, looking at her desperately and quivering.

"Hey, what's happened to you?" she cooed back and walked over. Kneeling down beside it, she stroked the cat's head, which left streaks of thin blood on her hand. "Jesus Christ." It whined again and then began to pant desperately; hyperventilating as it suffered some ambiguous torture. "Don't worry darling, come here, come here" she said, and placed the mutilated animal on the black apron covering her lap, where it curled into a ball and twitched "I'll call a vet."

By the time she had dialled the first four numbers, though, the cat had emitted its death rattle, and its head had flopped on her arm.

"Shit" she said, feeling tears well up in her eyes. Unsure of where to leave the limp feline corpse, she first tried to place it back between the bins, but, out of some strange reverence to an unknown but powerful code, she subsequently thought of placing it on top of the bin's lid before finally settling on the edge of a wall next to a patch of grass – telling herself that she would collect it in order to commemorate the universe's random violence later. She looked at it one final time, and curled it into a foetal position in an attempt to recoup some of its dignity.

"Get these on sodding platters and start passing them around," Derick snapped at her as she hurried inside, pointing aggressively at a baking tray covered in smoking canapés with the pair of tongs he was holding.

"Sorry... I... there was a cat... it..."

"I don't give a toss, the wanker said the queue word for us to start preparing a minute ago." Holding back tears, she started transferring the delicate little nests of duck from the rusty ovenware to sleek silverware with her slightly red fingers. Pushing the curtain aside just as the round of applause abated, she started brushing through the crowd and distributing the canapés. Among the first people to reach for one was the man wearing a lab coat who she had seen on her way out – now talking to a severely beautiful woman dripping in designer and diamonds near the entrance to the room.

"We've worked it out," he said, still panting a little.

"Get on with it – you can't be dressed like that here."

"They weren't eating its flesh. They were eating the plastic."

"What plastic?"

Still panting, "The… the plastic inside the cat… the microplastics… almost everything alive has them in… from packaging and waste… and when plastic starts to break down in the sea and gets into the drinking wat…"

"But the cat is dead?"

"Yes."

"Then there shouldn't be anything to worry about."

A few hours later, guests started adjusting collars and pulling at hems due to hot itches. Most of them left soon after.

About half an hour after the curtailed finishing time, A&E started getting calls and police started attending the sites of car crashes; where they checked vitals with ungloved hands.

By the early hours of the morning there was a lot of red on the marble walls of expensive houses, where the guests had kissed their children's sleeping foreheads before dropping dead.

Three days later, amidst a national epidemic, the last of the powder produced by the Mastics digesting the cat and the girls' bones blew away into the wind. Behind it, the plastic processing plant collapsed as the bacteria chomped their way to a cleaner world.

The Needs of the Few
Jennifer Rohn

Glass containers lined the bookshelves, stretching row upon row into the shadowy corners of the room. Centred in the window, the sun was just rising over the flat expanse of slate sea, the sky a hazy coral-bronze above. Directly below the back of the house the rocks tumbled down to the shore, impassable to anyone who might be curious enough to try to clamber up and spy inside.

It was going to be another scorcher, Rose observed. She'd have to be careful with the temperature in here today.

She approached the nearest row of containers, a haphazard collection of whatever she could get her hands on from the nearby recycling centre where she'd forged a financial relationship with the man in charge. As this man was not especially discreet, the whole town knew of the arrangement. She never actually heard the gossip, but she could imagine what they said: 'the sad lady doctor who'd lost her job at the big pharma company, a bit of a recluse, that one', 'maybe she's just a little crazy and collects jars instead of cats, or is stockpiling jam and chutney ahead of the Apocalypse, or is running a meth lab to make ends meet'.

In such a close-knit community, it was inevitable that a few people would work out what she was really up to. As so many had been touched personally by the Mandate, those who knew were supportive and had not reported her to the authorities – yet. Besides, some of these, or their relatives, had benefitted greatly from their discretion.

Rose peered into the nearest container, which had once held mayonnaise. Now it harboured a whirl of ochre-coloured matter fanned out over the jar's base, about an inch thick, with peaks and troughs like a baked meringue. Despite the lid, she could detect a faint whiff, something earthy and sour, both compelling and repellent at the same time. A layer of oily liquid had formed on top overnight – it would be ready for testing soon.

She took note of the jar's number, flipped a few pages in her coffee-stained notebook, and scribbled some observations. Then she moved on to the next container, home to an impressively hairy mauve-tinted infestation. Rose had read in history books that the early pioneers of this sort of endeavour had even pressed humble hospital bedpans into service, so she knew she was lucky to have such a bounty of glassware. One of the few good things about this wasteful society, she thought.

Sometimes the enormity of what she was doing would slap her in the face and she'd see it all with extra clarity, the rows of mismatched jars glinting in the light, the sheer diversity of the colourful stuff growing inside – cheerful pinks, evil-looking greens, muted oysters, lunar blues and every shade in between. Quirky, even beautiful. Such a far cry from her lab at Protectix Solutions, with its military-scale incubators, its stainless-steel bioreactors and fermenters, its robotic plating machines and the stacks of agar petri plates, date-stamped and ready-made from cases that appeared magically in the cold room. Nothing looked beautiful there, only matter-of-fact. Almost all of the manual labour had been replaced by technology – she'd felt like an acclaimed conductor, presiding over a clockwork-perfect orchestra of apparatus.

Here, her body ached from the non-stop work. Aside from the furtive glass scavenging and the constant washing and oven-sterilising, she was covered in cuts and bruises from harvesting a particular kind of algae twice daily from the slippery, barnacle-encrusted rocks when the tide receded. This she rendered in large vats to make a crude agar, which she spiked with beef broth and yeast before gelling it into yet more shallow bottles. These petridish substitutes were used for experiments in the conservatory, which on a sunny day would usually reach and retain a good temperature for incubation. The boiling algae imparted the house with a permanent briny smell that trumped the more exotic odours emanating from the mouldy jars. During the first few months she had been permanently sick, vomiting and shitting from whatever toxins had escaped their confines. Now, her body seemed to have come to an uneasy understanding with the menagerie under her care.

But far more than decent kit, ready-made agar plates and the cold sterility of proper health and safety provisions, she missed the company of colleagues. Science was never meant to be done alone. Even late at night or on weekends, there was always someone else knocking around at Protectix who could help pass the time with casual banter, or be persuaded down to the canteen for a midnight cup of tea and biscuits to celebrate a rare success or commiserate with over far more frequent failures. You could bounce crazy ideas around as you half-focused on whatever you were doing at the bench, manipulating machines with thoughtless ease – at the top of your game after decades of training. You felt you were in control, part of something greater. But here, the task was all-encompassing, leaving no time for hobbies or a social life. It was a blessing that she had so little mental space to reflect on what had brought her here, but she did regret the permanent lack of proper sleep. As it was, her life was governed by the tide tables and by the merciless microscopic overlords in their jars, warring it out endlessly, the killers and the killed.

It had all started off with the best of intentions, Rose knew all too well. 'Stewardship', it was called. A policy born of common sense. After all, the reason we were in this mess in the first place was because we had been too profligate with that precious gift to an undeserving humankind, determined to bungle its own salvation. Alexander Fleming, who had stumbled upon the lifesaving mould and its magic-bullet secretion back in the 1920s, had warned us to tread carefully, to dole it out sparingly, to use it only when absolutely necessary. His notes from the past read now like the tired and prophetic wisdom of a seasoned time-traveller.

But generation after generation, nobody listened to the father of antibiotics; or to those well-meaning public health authorities who likewise recognised the danger. The wonder drug was given away like sweets at the slightest cough, even for viral infections like the common cold against which antibiotics were useless. Some countries sold it over the counter for any hypochondriac to gorge upon, or allowed it to be hawked over the internet. The drugs were poured indiscriminately into animal feed and aquaculture until the entire planet was soaked in antibiotics. But then, all of the virgin bacteria in the world, like uncontacted Amazonian tribes suddenly beset by gunpowder, fought back with their own secret weapons: inborn genetic resistance to antibiotics, tidy cassettes of DNA over a billion years old that the bugs could switch on like a tap, modify to suit and pass around as easily as business cards. Unwittingly, humans helped bacteria to spread their resistance genes via crowded cities and transatlantic flights to every last corner of the globe: evolution did the rest.

One by one, the antibiotics stopped working – even the last-minute desperate efforts that were rushed out. But it was too little, too late. By the time the Scourge had evolved, there was only one useful drug left to fight it: Protectix's own star product, Mystamicin. It was an epidemic so swift and fatal that even the Americans, Chinese and Russians stopped squabbling and united with the others to hastily draw up the 'International Stewardship Accord Mandate of 2027'. ISAM, as it became known, was cruel and clinical, crafted in full knowledge that in order to save as many lives as possible, some would have to die. From that day forth, no antibiotics could be used for any infection that was 'not normally life-threatening'. Anyone prescribing antibiotics without permission would be arrested and thrown in jail. Misusing Mystamicin carried a life sentence.

After a few high-profile sentencings of brave doctors who refused to believe that the law would truly be enforced, the message sank in. Mystamicin was indeed in the process of saving the majority. But many thousands also perished from simple infections gone wrong, just as in the old days. Cuts from thorns. Unchecked urinary tract infections. Hip replacements. Chronic coughs whose bearers were too weak to shake them off. The media was incentivised by the government not to dwell on the collateral damage, but word of mouth – a social media far older and more resilient – kept grim tabs. It was a bitter irony: people prayed for a diagnosis of the Scourge, or something equally deadly like meningitis, but not the potential death sentence of an infected bedsore.

Rose had quit her job at Protectix out of protest, part of a wave of resignations across the global healthcare system that did not change anything. She had not trained and sacrificed for thirty years to let people die from curable bacterial infections. Then, later, after she emerged from her own personal hell to find that she was still alive, still angry, and still dedicated to saving lives, she moved to the other end of the country, sank her entire life savings into the dilapidated beach house and set up shop.

"I heard you heal the sick," the woman said, holding a bundle in her arms.

"Come in," Rose said. "Let me see."

Maxine, Rose's neighbour, handed over the bundle with trembling arms. Rose parted the cotton folds to reveal the infant: pale and clammy, unresponsive, breathing rapidly and shallowly. She drew in her breath at the gash on his forehead, vivid red against the stitches and oozing yellow pus.

"He fell over on the back patio," Maxine said. "He's two years old – he hasn't been walking long. I only turned my back for a moment…" Her voice caught, and she paused to compose herself. "The doctor said it was quite deep, but would likely clear on its own, if I kept it clean."

'Likely.' A causal throw of the dice, of calculated risk, that had become the new normal.

"This was when?" Rose struggled to filter the anger from her own voice, but it welled up inside like magma.

"Three days ago. Yesterday, he started being… off, and the wound got worse. And now, this rash…"

"But surely you could go back to the doctor. I'm no clinician, but this looks very much like sepsis. He should qualify for urgent antibiotics now."

Maxine twisted her hands together. "I did try, but the waitlist for ISAM Appeals is a couple of days. I entered his name, but I'm worried he doesn't have that long."

Rose didn't say that she was right to be worried. Instead: "I'll treat him. But you need to know what you're signing up for."

"I'll pay anything!"

Rose knew that Maxine was a renowned local homeopathic 'healer' who peddled useless remedies from her front parlour and was well-compensated for her efforts. It must have cost her a great deal of pride to come knocking on Rose's door.

"My treatments are free," Rose said quietly. But there were things Maxine needed to understand. That Rose didn't have the technology available to analyse which antibiotics were being produced. She scavenged microbes from every available surface: from soils, from plants, from the wet beach sand, from the rock pools at low tide, from puddles and shellfish and clay. These she grew on the shelves in bottles until they'd formed a thick growth of mould or bacteria. Using the clean agar bottles, she'd test their secretions on samples taken from the patient, to see if anything would kill the infection.

She was flying blind: she didn't know if the secretions contained any killer chemicals or, if they did, whether she was isolating a known antibiotic like penicillin against which the infection would be long-since resistant, or something new that the infection had never seen before and might respond to. At Rose's lowly pay grade, she had not been privy to the secret of Mystamicin's source material, though rumour said it came from the sea – one of the last untapped microbiological frontiers. There was no quality control, no animal testing, no clinical trials: just a raw potion injected intravenously by a person unqualified to do so, a once-in-a-lifetime concoction that could never be replicated exactly even if it did work.

To underscore her point, Rose sketched to Maxine what had happened when Howard Florey and his colleagues had conducted the first trial of penicillin back in 1940: the patient had responded well, but they'd run out of the scarce drug and he eventually relapsed and died. So there might not be enough of her drug to control the infection, or it might cause deadly side effects or allergic reactions. Rose hadn't killed any of her patients yet, but it was probably only a matter of time, and she needed to be sure that Maxine understood the risks.

"I'm a mother," Maxine said flatly. "A mother can tell when her child is dying. Besides, I peddle untested potions for a living." Despite everything, a twitch of a smile, of embarrassed self-knowledge. "Do your worst, Doc."

Rose had laboured all day, inoculating tiny amounts of pus harvested from the injury into dozens of clean agar bottles. As the case was so urgent, she couldn't waste time culturing the bacteria properly, coddling it over a few days into a nice lawn of growth that would make the subsequent testing easier. Instead, she smeared each test antibiotic right alongside the smear of pus and hoped that any effects would be obvious the next morning. The conservatory would retain its heat long into the night, fostering bacterial growth, so by morning there might be some clarity.

Her sleep was rough, broken. Just before dawn, she slipped into dreams. Lily, as always, was holding her small hand against Rose's cheek and studying her with earnest blue eyes: "It's not your fault, Mama."

Rose dragged herself awake and went straight to the conservatory. The pus from the boy's wound had grown nicely into streaks of custard-coloured dots. Occasionally she wasn't able to coax the tiny predators into life at all – many bugs just didn't like her primitive algae and broth concoction. But this one did, and it looked like a common Staphylococcus – she knew its odour of faint rot well – and didn't need to bother working it up to confirm with her microscope. Anyway, it didn't really matter what its name was, only if it had any vulnerabilities.

She picked up each bottle in turn, feeling that tingle of excitement that most scientists never lose, no matter how experienced or jaded. Form a hypothesis, do the experiment, record the result. Most of the bottles were unpromising – the Staph had steamrollered over its mouldy adversary as if it were harmless seawater. But one of the bottles – wait.

She held it up to the growing daylight. There was a zone of clear agar between the Staph and the mould substance – a battleground where the Staph had lost and been forced to retreat. A swathe of destruction, in short, that Alexander Fleming would have instantly recognised.

Full of triumph, Rose spent a few hours propagating the original mould – a fuzzy grey specimen scraped from the putrid body of a squid washed up on shore and covered with flies, her notes reminded her – into many dozens of bottles, just in case the child responded to the first dose. It would be touch and go if she could grow enough in time, but this mould had flourished briskly and just might win the race.

The ringtone shattered the funereal hush of the house: Maxine, letting her know, as her voice choked with emotion, that her son was responding, pulling through. That he was going to make it. The doctor had praised his 'unusually resilient immune system' – and didn't have any suspicions, thank goodness. Her secret was safe. Could she make a cash donation to the cause, anything at all?

After hanging up the phone, limp with relief, Rose hesitated by her bedroom door. There was no time to lose – she was behind on her algae collection, and a kitchen-full of rank bottles needed cleaning. Instead, she stepped inside, pulled open the bottom dresser drawer and took out the shoebox. She hadn't looked for more than a year, as if pretending it did not exist could possibly seal her heart against the unspeakable tragedy within.

Off came the lid. The tiny slippers, like furry rabbit tails, piercing her like an arrow. The lock of hair, copper-coloured and as shiny as the day she'd snipped it. The hand-knitted sweater, so small it folded into the palm of her hand. The tears flowed, blurring tiny footprints in clay, a crayon drawing of a family of three stick figures with impossibly long arms and legs holding hands. She untied the pink ribbon from the stack of photographs: various stages of Lily, from babyhood until aged six, and from then no further. She'd saved only one picture of Dario after he fled – the three of them, hopelessly happy and completely clueless about what lay ahead. And finally, at the very bottom. The official letter, headed from the department of ISAM:

Name: Lily Grace Foster. Diagnosis: bacterial chest infection (ISAM grade 2). Decision: Not normally life-threatening: No recourse to Mystamicin.

That evening, she slipped out of the house and went down to the rocks, where high tide pounded. She saw no one walking the bluffs to either side – it was that time when families were tired from too much sun, sand and sea, and gathered together to regroup, to eat, to love. When houses light up against the gathering darkness, turned inward, safe in the present and heedless of what might one day come. She could hear larks in the dune grasses, swifts high above and the endless taunting of the gulls. The offshore breeze was fresh and vital, sucked from the cooling earth. Behind her, the sun angled down, and ahead, the water reflected back silvery blue and tangerine. Just a few more minutes before the tide turned.

She pulled the letter out of her pocket, ripped it into tiny pieces and let them flutter away in the wind.

The War That Ended Yesterday
David Turnbull

Part One

"What do you remember about the war?"

"What war?"

"The one that ended yesterday."

"I don't remember a war."

"Excellent."

"Who was it between?"

"We are the victors. You are the vanquished."

"Am I a prisoner?"

"There is no need to imprison you. You are defeated and subjugated. You pose no threat."

"How can you be so certain?"

"What do you remember about the war?"

"Nothing. Nothing at all."

"You were neutralised by superior weaponry of a biological nature. We released a virus which wiped the memory of enemy combatants."

"I was a combatant? Is that how I came to lose my arm?"

"Don't trouble yourself over such trivial matters. As a consequence of the virus post-traumatic stress is rendered impotent. You will not experience any anxiety as a consequence of unpleasant flashbacks."

"And I'm not a prisoner?"

"There is no need. There will be no resistance or insurrection. The virus has seen to it that not one of you remember what you were fighting for."

"Is my country under occupation?"

"Your country is now our country. You are a blank sheet of paper, my friend. You will soon adopt our traditions, our institutions and religious mores. Another benefit of the virus. Cultural and political imperialism writ large."

"Were we so different?"

"Don't trouble yourself with such matters. We are selecting a wife and children for you."

"A wife and children?"

"Millions died in the conventional war before we released the virus. Widows and orphans abound."

"Don't they remember the war?"

"Once we had neutralised the combatants we detonated moisture bombs containing the virus into the atmosphere above your towns and cities. It rained amnesia."

"Did I have a wife and children? Are they dead?"

"Do you remember a wife and children?"

"No."

"Then don't trouble yourself with such matters."

"Do I have a name? I can't remember my name."

"A name is being selected for you. One which blends with our culture."

"Where will I live? Where will I work?"

"Homes are being rebuilt. We are engaged in an extensive reconstruction project. There will be work for all."

"Why all the reconstruction?"

"Because of the war. There was a considerable amount of destruction caused by blanket bombing in the early stages."

"What war?"

"The war that ended yesterday."

"I don't remember a war."

"Excellent."

Part Two

"What do you remember about the war?"

"What war?"

"The war that you won."

"We won a war?"

"Not we as in us. You were the victors. We were the vanquished."

"I don't remember a war."

"Excellent. That's the effect of the virus."

"Virus? What virus?"

"The one that you developed as a biological weapon so that you could defeat and subjugate us. The one that caused us to forget."

"I don't understand."

"The virus infects the brain – destroys the cells which store memory. It makes you forget who you are. It robs you of your history and all that you hold precious."

"I truly don't recall any of this."

"That's because you have been infected. You crowed too much about your victory. We pieced the evidence together. Figured out who we were. And how we might seize back what was rightfully ours. How we might defeat our oppressor."

"I'm infected? You've wiped my memory? How?"

"We stole supplies of the virus from your stockpiles. Poisoned the water supply. Hoarded our own water for months beforehand to protect ourselves."

"Am I a prisoner?"

"There is no need. You have forgotten everything. Do you feel a desire for revenge?"

"I feel nothing."

"Point proven, then."

"But what is to stop us doing the same thing to you? Now that you've told me all of this – what is to stop the war from perpetuating, tit for tat?"

"We are taking precautions."

"In what way?"

"By using the virus to the advantage of all. We intend to finally extinguish the causes of the war."

"What war?"

"The one that ended yesterday – for the second time. Both sides will forget when we share this simple jug of water."

"One jug – and one jug alone – can do this?"

"Millions of jugs, my friend. Being shared this moment across the land you occupied and the land that was once your own."

"Did we not once drink alcohol to forget?"

"Perhaps."

"But in the morning, we remembered."

"Take your glass, comrade. Help me to pour. I only have one arm. I don't remember how that happened and therefore I harbour no malice. Let us drink and toast our future."

L-One-LY Virus
Jessica Laine

He withdrew from her, became limp, cold, and then lifeless.

"God damn it, I hadn't expected him to have it," Z half whispered to herself. After all, they met outside of the portal having a short but earnest conversation. He actually looked at her, and commented on her mysterious eyes, giving her the rare signal that it might be okay to lure him home and that maybe he was capable and clean.

It had never gone this far before, and she was foolish to have let it.

Had she been with him long enough to become infected? Or was she the infected one, unknowingly killing the poor chap? Probably the latter. There had been other attempts to get close to someone, to find an immune among the outbreak, and yet she had always been the one to survive. Why? She did not know.

In a panic, she ordered an antiseptic shower, antiviral and anti-bacterial therapies, a vaginal microbiome transplant, an extra order of methyl donor injections, the evacuation of his body, and whiskey.

Waiting, she reached between her thighs to check for any evidence of him and perhaps the rare opportunity to sneak an undetected sample, but there was nothing. Typical. Her body was void of the warmth aftermath, sticky residue of elation. Even the air was vacant. There was no sweet emulsion of spit and sweat; only the common, stale, insipid nothingness.

Rolling over, she mirrored his disengagement, and was faced with the familiar emptiness. This was what was left of us all: hollow orgasms, uninhabited hearts, invalid lives, and now these 'mysterious' deaths of the once immortal.

"What irony," she exclaimed to the cold ears of the cadaver beside her. She imagined the melancholy life he had muddled through on a daily basis. "In seeking vitality you perished." At least he tried; effort that most would not dream of.

The cleaners took him away, sterilised her and her dome, and cleared Z of immediate infection. In the refuge, she was alone again. She sighed in relief, for what if he had not been infected? He would still be beside her – then what? What would two humans even do in the company of one another?

She took out her notebook and added him to the tally of death tolls. But his cause of death was marked with a rare diagnosis of attempted sexual intimacy. Other notes of the deceased included: a handshake, prolonged eye contact, conversation not through the code, and so on. With each strike of her pen she felt more connected to them, the dash marked ghosts hovering over the pages of data that lead to null conclusions. Ghosts could not tell her their stories and the secrets behind this seemingly fable-like disease. Haunted she was, but Z chose this path, a risky career, aiming to defeat the virus.

At first it was impersonal, and she treated the work like any job. Day to day she attempted to collect more data, find those uninfected, take samples, study the pathogenesis of the disease, work in the lab to replicate the virus in cells and animal models, but then she started liking the rare, but brief, moments of intimacy and human connection and became obsessed with a cure for reasons beyond a pay check. But Z had not got very far in her mission, and the work, like life, was a solo effort – or so she thought. Agency employees did not know anything about other workers and there was no interaction. There were notes shared from time to time, but even this was coded and could not be linked to a person, for it was too risky.

They knew little about the virus: its manifestation was unknown even to the infected. The moment it was activated, people's capillaries became intoxicated, and they choked on invisible poison that clogged and restricted their arteries, instantaneously stopping their hearts. They became the impossible, the mortal, a feat rewarded with an immediate certificate of death – where they joined other legends.

At first it was the big acts of intimacy that led to these rare cases of mortality. Seemingly normal behaviours such as sex (with or without an orgasm) and birth (in the rare cases that pregnancy had occurred) became momentous suicidal acts which lead to what became known as instant mortal syndrome, or L virus for short. Begrudgingly, we began to avoid these acts, but then it started happening with any act of intimacy such as laughter, a hug, crying, sharing, dancing, and smiling... So we stopped engaging in any form of affection and intimacy with any other human being. Oddly, our survival depended on disconnection and isolation, and yet it was not a hard adjustment to make for we had already established a baseline of disconnection from each other.

We were immortal, and had become the Gods that those foolish past humans wasted their lives paying homage to. But we could not maintain such a hierarchical state without consequences, as evolution would have it. We started to become so individualised that there was no we, only mes and Is. Is that became so self-absorbed that they were unable to see any other being.

However, there were those that were driven to try to salvage the natural affinity for a tribe, maybe because of the desire for companionship or to escape the state of madness experienced from the everlasting disconnect. And Z was one of those. She joined the agency to find a cure, taking risks with every data point, for Z believed we could no longer live in our self-contained bubbles, temporarily satisfied by the digital devices we glorified.

The next morning she woke in a sweat, but fortunately her vitals were still clear. She logged in to the macrodatabase to write up the observations of her deadbeat date from last night and check for any other agents' notes. There was nothing profound other than incident case reports, all lacking a link to potential mechanism.

Moving on to look for more uninfected, Z decided the best option was to go to the strip, a probable place for an encounter. But she spotted no one. Getting cases was an arduous process: people stayed in their pods, wore glasses to shield eye contact in the portal; most simply stayed at home in their glorified mirages of life.

Suddenly there was a breath so close that it lifted the hairs on her neck. A man's voice asked if she wanted a sip of warmth. He wafted a flask of something that smelled like old-timey gasoline in front of her. Reluctantly, she took it.

She couldn't make out his face or deduce why he was talking to her, as all she could think was that he should be dead by now.

"I know why L virus developed, and how to cure it," he boldly claimed. "We became collectively separate. Using devices and technologies as a replacement for any and all face-to-face interaction. We then broke up the sexes, subdivided our homes…"

"Yeah… but it was progress," was all she could muster.

"Of course, the perfect virtual partners were exciting and parthenogenesis gave women more freedom, especially after sending the offspring away to the camps to train to be the best and fittest. But all acts became isolated. How then were we to know how to interact?"

She could feel his intensity strengthen with every word.

"Now any interaction kills us. Our bodies cannot tolerate the emotion. We surpassed our societal evolutionary needs for collaboration or even reproduction, for fuck's sake."

She was taken aback at how well these phrases mimicked her every thought.

"Do you think it is the act of intimacy itself that kills us or is it that those who are intimate transmit the virus?" Z asked the common stranger.

No one knew this, and there was little way to test it.

"There's one way to find out."

He reached for her hand, but Z felt her chest tighten, she did not want a repeat of last night, or worse, to know what would happen if they were capable of connection. She ran, and did not look back until she reached the portal.

She felt him through her, and she wanted all of him and nothing at the same time.

But it did not kill her. Perhaps there was a chance to break the isolation.

Or perhaps feeling anything was too much, and she, we, and I would remain a victim of L-one-ly.

Transmissions from the Vitality Pod
Dan Coxon

7.17.56

Three injections today. Two in my arm, one in my right eyeball. It stings for a minute, but the unit is efficient in spraying for infection. Seven pills, most of which I can't identify. The largest is green and shaped like a bullet. I can't help wondering if it's meant to be inserted somewhere. Once I've swallowed them, my wrist monitor flashes for a moment, then settles on 127. Not bad, but could be better. Via iShare, Marcus boasts that his is up to 136, a full nine years more than mine. I'll hit the gym later.

The pod's white light gives me a headache by lunchtime, but my unit is efficient in dosing me with painkillers. I don't check which ones. I manage a new personal best on the rowing machine, competing against a virtual team from the late twentieth century, so I celebrate with a sparkling aloe juice as the light fades into evening settings. Wrist still says 127. Must try harder tomorrow.

7.18.56

Six pills today, four injections. The extra one has been scheduled by my unit as I have to go Outside this afternoon. I have my suit, naturally, but the idea of the Outside stresses me. My blood pressure has gone up. The unit says not to worry, it has a pill for that. Even so, my wrist monitor has slumped to 124 by breakfast, and I can practically feel those three years being whittled away by the anxiety. This meeting had better be worth it. It's just like the Shanghai office to feel they need to conduct the transaction face to face, an actual signature on actual paper. It all feels so mid-twentieth century.

I spend ten minutes making sure the suit is fully sealed before opening the door. There's a hiss as it slides back, and I imagine I can see the particles of dirt drifting through from the Outside. It reminds me that I'll need to fumigate once I get back. I set a reminder.

It's been almost six months since I was Outside. I've seen the security cam images of course, and the drone broadcasts. The masses of poor clustered around open fires, their faces blackened with dirt and soot. The drones picked up footage of a small boy last week, only five or six, foraging in the waste cans two blocks from here. Shots of him tugging with his teeth at the skin and bones of an old chicken wing, scraping blue mould from a block of cheese before wolfing it down in three ravenous bites. I can't remember the last time I saw mould.

None of it prepares me for the reality as the second airlock door opens. There are a few of them a couple of metres beyond my door, their bodies hunched under layers of synthetic wool. They stand as soon as they see me, their hands held out, pleading. One, a scarf wrapped around the lower half of his face, has open sores from his fingertips to his wrists. The news broadcasts claim that medical supplies are dropped off on street corners once a week, but I hear rumours that they stopped over a year ago. Certainly, the man with the sores can't be following any of the approved skin care plans.

I do my best to step around them, thumbing the suit's defence net to 'on'. A couple of them receive minor shocks as I stride past, so I tell the suit to play some Wagner, loud, until we're past them. I don't mind the electric crackle, but the screams are too much. I can feel my stress levels rocketing just at the thought of it.

At the corner the crowd clears, and I stop for a breather by a rusted metal drum. It looks like someone has been using it as a fire pit, the edges scorched and blackened. I check my wrist. I thought so – down to 122 in a matter of minutes. If I was still in my pod I'd be wiping my brow, but the suit just wicks it away, reuses it for the built-in cooling system. Thank God for technology.

It's as I step away that it happens. I'm not sure what it means at first, but suddenly there are red lights flashing across my visor, and Ride of the Valkyries is abruptly interrupted by an ear-piercing digital klaxon. My heart rate spikes almost immediately. I stagger with the sensory overload – and it's then that I spot it. At the back of my leg, my calf, the suit has caught on a jagged spur sticking out from the side of the drum. From ankle to knee, in one great, obscene rip, the outer lining is torn, open to the air, to the dirt, the dust, the germs. I'm no longer sealed in. I am Outside.

The sweat breaks for real now as I sprint back the way I came. The Shanghai office be damned. I'm not sure if I'm imagining it, but I swear I can feel a prickling sensation along the back of my leg, like a thousand tiny spiders racing across my skin. There's a physical shiver in reaction, but, more than that, my brain won't let it go. I picture the germs feasting as I run, drinking my sweat and breeding, spreading, infecting as they go. The taste of vomit rises in my throat.

Thankfully, all those hours on the treadmill pay off and I'm able to shoulder my way past the growing mass of bodies in front of my door. The man with the scarf around his face reaches out an open hand so I punch him, hard, in his sore-covered face, stunning him with the electric-blue crackle of my suit's defences so that I can slip past. I jab at the entry button, hear the hiss of the airlock door behind me, collapse into the pod. Pulling off the suit I order an immediate fumigation, and more pills, more shots. Anything the pod can give me.

While I wait, I cough, and look at my hand in dread.

7.19.56

I've calmed down a little now. The pod has given me something for that – said I needed it for my blood pressure. Everything feels kind of fuzzy, which is nice. I think I smell lavender.

On iShare, Marcus says that something similar happened to him last year, on a trip to the Exchange. And he's up to 137 now, so it's clearly not done him much harm.

As for me, I can't quite see my wrist monitor properly. Everything looks blurred, the focus softened by the meds. I thought it said 107 earlier, but it looks different now. Are there only two digits? One of them might be a six.

The pod offers me another two pills, yellow, with smiling faces printed on them. I swallow them gratefully. Everything's going to be just fine.

Inside the Locked Cupboard
Pippa Goldschmidt

I thought I understood how it was all going to work. I thought I could predict my future, just like I've been successful at predicting the outcomes of experiments. Well, I was wrong, wasn't I?

The first day was so satisfying. When I arrived, the staff and post-docs and students were gathered together in the main lab in their freshly laundered and uniformly white lab coats. All in honour of me.

Oh, I knew there were issues I was going to have to get to grips with. One of the most successful fruit fly labs in the country, producing some of the best and most innovative work, and yet something wasn't quite right. I'd been warned about the procedures not followed, things being allowed to get rather lax. Essential information gone astray and all that old equipment piling up in the corners of the labs. And the books! Volume upon volume of discredited ideas like Lamarckism and Lysenkoism. I tried to donate them to the University library, but I just got a tartly worded refusal in reply, so I'm afraid they went to the dump.

Besides, there were more important things to be worrying about than a pile of old books. I had an idea and I knew we could do it here. It would save a huge amount of time and money, and put an end to all that carping about the experiments not being carried out correctly. I was going to replace the flies with a virtual model; FRUITY. Instead of having a room full of thousands of flies that took up space and had to be fed and looked after, we would have a computer fly that anyone could mutate as they liked, and then examine the outcomes. Why not? I knew people in the astrophysics department never bothered going to cold mountain-top telescopes any more to observe the night sky, they just created simulations of it in the comfort of their own warm offices. We would do something similar. After all, a fly is simpler than a universe.

The Board agreed with me: it was the reason why I was offered the job. But first, the actual fly room had to be dismantled and everything had to be rationalised.

As part of this process, some of the post-docs were tasked with the disposal of the flies. I spent a bit of time watching them do this, standing outside the fly room, checking that the flies were adequately doped before being tipped into the flasks of ethanol. The post-docs never acknowledged me watching them through the glass wall, they were too busy, too focused on their work. But I noticed that they always smiled as they dropped the flies down the funnel into the flask. Small, secret smiles. It was unsettling. Perhaps it was the first indication that things might not go the way I'd planned.

As the first woman to head up a lab in such an ancient, prestigious institution I wanted all the signs to be changed to reflect this. Senior management agreed: nobody wanted it to be 'Professor Miller's lab' any more. People stopped calling it that straight away, as if they couldn't wait to dump his name into the dustbin of out-of-date scientists.

Unlike him, I'm not a professor. I may have spent more of my professional life in tedious bureaucracy than I would have liked, I may have missed out on the glory of first-authored Nature papers, but I've done all right, and if that wretched admin post in the research council was the price I had to pay to get any sort of job at all after my maternity leave, then fair enough. I'd got my reward now.

Dr MacMillan's Lab.

It has a nice look to it, doesn't it?

So why did the sodding signs keep changing? Why did some of the letters keep fading away? The official explanation was that it was a problem with the new printer toner that the University powers-that-be insisted on us using. Less toxic, better for the environment. I was all for that, of course, but why was it that the only letters that remained, the only ones that anyone could still read, were:

Mill's Lab.

As if to announce to the world that he hadn't quite gone away – that he'd simply mutated into another form.

One of the hurdles of moving to a computer-based approach for the flies was the network itself. Just after we got the beta version of FRUITY up and running, the network started to struggle. It was taking an age to open any new files, and deleted files kept mysteriously reappearing. I called a meeting with the head of computer services to get to the bottom of this, but the woman seemed oddly anxious, playing with a paperclip throughout the entire discussion, bending the thin metal into contorted shapes as she explained how every file on the network must remain accessible at all times. 'For safety reasons', she said.

'Safety?' I was baffled. She looked embarrassed when she left my office, dropping pieces of broken paperclip onto my desk.

I asked my admin assistant if he knew anything about this. He pursed his lips, and took some time before replying.

"The Prof. had been accustomed to downloading some unusual material off the internet and onto the lab network. He claimed it was for research. The police took a rather keen interest in it."

Now I understood why none of us here could delete anything. Thousands upon thousands of files on the network, with more files generated by our work every day. Consequently, my computer was so slow the damn thing hardly managed to crawl its way through the essential processes. It was rather ironic in a lab that had become famous for demonstrating the contribution of cell death to the development of living organisms. Famous for experiments showing how attributes like wings and legs are formed as a result of apoptosis, certain cells dying in the developing embryo. And we were surrounded by all these undead, zombie-like files clogging up the network.

But the discovery of the real reason for my predecessor's hasty retirement also explained another unusual feature of my office: the glass walls. As I sit here looking at spreadsheet after spreadsheet and trying to make our budget stretch a little further, I'm always aware of people walking along the corridor, looking in.

Which other room in this lab has glass walls?

The fly room.

The end of the actual fly room meant some of the post-docs had to be let go. I selected one and emailed her, asking her to come and see me.

Even though I offered to write her a good reference and put her in touch with heads of other labs, she didn't take it well. "Why me?" she muttered. She had very curly hair, I couldn't help noticing, as her curls shook when she covered her face and wept.

The next day, I went to the fly room and stood outside, watching a post-doc peering into a flask. It was Curly Hair, so I opened the door and entered.

I told her again how sorry I was.

She said she didn't know what I was talking about.

"Yesterday morning," I said, "I know it must be a shock to you, and I'm so sorry. It was a random decision, not at all based on your individual characteristics."

"Characteristics?" She gazed at me, a fly gripped in her tweezers before she dropped it into the flask and we both watched it sink. "You've got the wrong person," she said, and smiled because she'd just killed the fly.

Now we come to the cupboard. The cupboard that sits in the corner of my office. I never had any use for it because I prefer open shelves for all my books and papers, so I asked the admin assistant to get rid of it. But he said he couldn't because it wasn't on the University's register and therefore, technically, it didn't exist. He told me he could add it and it would have to be on the register for ten days before it could be taken away.

This was the Professor's cupboard. His private cupboard. What did he use it for?

All over the world our collaborators were keenly following the developments of FRUITY and the easiest way to keep them informed was via Buzz!, the specially designed social media platform for biologists in our discipline. I got into the habit of buzzing a few times each day to remind everyone of the advantages of working with simulations of flies, and how easier it would be for people who aren't particularly dexterous or who have vision problems. The buzz box would pop up on my screen and I would spend a happy hour answering queries.

I rarely make any real effort to get more followers on Buzz!. I don't believe it has that much impact on our REF in spite of what people claim. So I was surprised to see the number of followers increasing.

But the avatars of these new followers were all depictions of fruit fly mutants. My followers weren't real people, they were flies. Zombie flies, eggbox flies, hologram flies et cetera, and all of them were forwarding my buzzes to each other, back and forth as if they were in some sort of echo chamber. It had to be a student prank. The students must have created a bot to do this – it was the sort of tedious nonsense they'd find amusing. But it was annoying because very quickly all my real followers were drowned out by the fly avatars.

I signed off Buzz!, hoping for a respite in the real world. In spite of its glass walls, my office is my sanctuary. Only a few more days before I could get rid of the cupboard. I emailed my assistant to remind him about it.

Today was the day that the cupboard was due to be removed, and FRUITY is scheduled to come online next week. I signed onto Buzz! to give people the details of how they can access the model and create their own mutations. But before I started to write a new buzz, I checked on my followers. The number had grown exponentially and all of them had fly avatars. Small pictures of flies with no head or deformed wings filled my screen. Even when I shut my eyes, I could hear a buzzing, as if my new followers were right here in my office, talking about me. The numbers of them… they're breeding online. Perhaps this means that they'll die off after a few weeks, just like real flies. Perhaps.

The cupboard in the corner of the office is still here. Monolithic, silent. I can't imagine anyone will actually turn up here and get rid of it. It looks like it will be here for ever, long after the rest of us.

The flies on Buzz! are talking to each other. They're asking 'what happened to the fly room?' and 'is that why we're here and not in the fly room?'

Are they the avatars of the dead flies?

My assistant tells me there's been a mistake and the cupboard will have to stay here for some time while he sorts it out. An error in the registry. I wave him away. I'm not interested. Now the avatars are talking about the flask, about being dropped into the flask and drowned. Oh God, this is horrible. All my other followers are drifting away. I've had almost no interactions with them this week about FRUITY. The fly avatars are scaring them away.

I give up on Buzz! and go back to my spreadsheet. As I sit at my desk, staring at my screen and trying to get Excel to work properly (which of course it won't, because of the network problems) I'm aware of people passing by outside my office, looking in at me. I never catch their faces; I never even see anything of them apart from their white lab coats but I know they're there.

I glance away so often from the computer screen and the spreadsheet that I keep losing my place in those minute numbers and I have to start all over again, my eyes crawling around the screen trying to find the right cell. I know I have to delete a row but the spreadsheet freezes yet again. Even the mouse is stationary. Now, nothing at all in this office is moving.

I sit, waiting.

A fly appears in front of me and lands on the computer screen. I'm thankful for it, watching it as it zig-zags in front of one spreadsheet cell to another, partially covering the numbers. It's just me and the fly in here, and I breathe a bit easier because it feels better than being distracted by the fly avatars. The fly leaves the screen, and I can't see it any more. A tiny loss, but a loss all the same.

I get up from my desk and walk across the office until I reach the cupboard. I crouch down in front of it, examining its doors, until I'm lying down stretched out on the floor and I am finally invisible to everyone else.

I glance at the cupboard doors, one of them is just slightly open and inside it's completely dark. A darkness free of spreadsheets and post-docs and fly avatars. A darkness separate from the light shining down on the flies drowning in the flask. I want more of the darkness to counteract the relentless glass and reflections of this place. I open the door a bit wider.

Inside the cupboard are rows of box files, the sort that every academic uses for their papers and notes. I peer closer. In the gloom of the cupboard it's difficult to see very much, but now I can make out some faint writing on each of the box files' labels;

Mill

Part of my predecessor's name.

Or mine.

I inch closer to the box files, they belong to me now, and I do the only thing I can do – the thing I've been trained to do. I reach for the nearest box file and, while still hidden from view from everyone beyond the glass, I pull it towards me.

It weighs less than it should do if there were papers inside. When I shake it I can hear something rustle like fallen leaves, before the lid opens up and reveals the secrets of the box. It's not what I was expecting, there are no piles of yellowed journal articles nor old exam scripts. Inside this box are corpses. An uncountable number of dead bodies. They must have been accumulated over many experiments, over a very long period of time.

I bury my hands in the mound of shining flies. They brush softly against my fingertips and a few of them spill onto the carpet. There is something both terrifying and beautiful in the sheer quantity of death. I know my predecessor felt the same way about these flies. Is that why he kept them to himself rather than abandoning them in the fly room?

Finally – this. A single living fly rises up from the box. How can it have survived? But it takes to the air, and I watch it for as long as possible as it flies from my office and into the corridor, and only then do I wish it luck.

CHOLESTEROL5.9, BigFLY
Antoine Saint Honoré

BigFLY likes to sit on the back of my hand. I like to watch BigFLY's mandible. BigFLY is 8cms long and 6cms wide. My BigFLY is standard BigFLY size. BigFLY comes from space.

"You make sure your BigFLY doesn't bother other passengers," says conductor with wink.

He straps me in tight. SkyTRAIN takes 8 minutes from deepKENT to London. I love SkyTRAIN. I always make calculation. If I am in the toilet I count the tiles. If I see windows I count them. SkyTRAIN has 12 carriages. Each carriage has 20 rows. Each row has 28 seats. One SkyTRAIN takes 6720 people. SkyTRAIN system is 3 trains wide. SkyTRAIN runs every 60 seconds. In one hour SkyTRAIN takes 403,200 people from deepKENT to London. Also SkyTRAIN goes from deepCAMBS and SkyTRAIN deepWest. RushLOVE lasts from 5am to 8.30am. So SkyTRAIN takes 10.5 million people to London each RUSH. But says 10 million on touchWALL. So WALL is wrong.

We live in NewPandaTower, deepKENT 11. Tower is 56 levels. Each level 125 flats. 5800 people average. 27 Towers in deepKENT2 NewPandaTOWN. Our tower is most osharey says Daddy. We have garden and swimming pools on the roof. Never talk about money says Daddy. It's not polite. BigFLY likes to swim in the pool but he is banned. We got a message in boxBOX saying residents COMMz ask children to keep BigFLY out of pools, ohuru and naked areas. I want to obey but I like to keep

BigFLY with me always. I stroke BigFLY. When I stroke BigFLY he moves his mandibles.

BigFLY comes from space. Prime Minister HeadINABOX700 says no one knows where BigFLY comes from and we have to be careful. Daddy says HeadINABOX has to say something. Every day Daddy brings home cake. Daddy is cakechef artist. BigFLY likes Mont Blanc. He likes Chestnut cream.

47cup gave me BigFLY. 47cup is my best friend. I love 47cup. He lives in realLONDON. 47cup found 10 BigFLIES in the park and they all came home with him. He gave one to me after Treasure of the House killed my first BigFLY. He said BigFLY was disgusting. I said to him "You should touch him. You will see space." But he said "He is disgusting" and treaded on him and killed him. I cried and Daddy told him off. I told 47cup my baby brother kill BigFLY and 47cup gave me a new BigFLY. They all came to him in the park, he said. He said we can go to the park together and see if more BigFLYs come but I said its OK because one was enough. You only need one BigFLY. Nearly all the children in my school have BigFLY.

The Government in SMALLSMALLHux want to ban BigFLY. They take them away and kill them. But more BigFLY keep coming. Government in LOVE-LOVE-ENGLAND say BigFLY is legal. Daddy asks questions about BigFLY. Daddy likes to stroke BigFLY. He says he feels peaceful when he touches BigFLY. But Treasure of the House won't touch BigFLY. He says he is disgusting.

I love Skytrain. Skytrain travels at 386.9 KMH. BigFLY scared at 345KMH. I stroke BigFLY to let him know it's OK. They let us take BigFLY into school. At first BigFLY was banned but HeadInABOX made announcement and said OK. Anyway BigFLY just float outside window and looked in. Teacher said Government scientists did experiments and find no danger so BigFLY is OK. But other passengers they don't like BigFLY.

Some people try and kill BIgFLY and stand on them and kill them but more BigFLY always comes so even if people kill them there are always more BigFLY. They like to be a pet.

BigFLY comes from space. Scientists say they don't know where BigFLY comes from. Teacher says there are more than 750 million BigFLY on Earth. I always make calculations. BigFLY has life expectancy of 10 months. 47cup says we will keep BigFLY in a closed room in his flat and see if they breed. No one knows where BigFLY comes from.

In my dream I am touching BigFLY. I stroke his back. When I wake up BigFLY is next to my bed. He likes to sleep next to WakeUpBaby. He lets me stroke his back. When I stroke his back I see space. This morning there were stars. First time I see stars. This morning the space had cuts. Seven stars in each cut. The cuts in rows. I counted 478 rows up and 356 rows across. I calculate 1191176 stars in 14 seconds I had my eyes closed touching BigFLY.

I played football today at school. BigFLY likes to watch. He hovers over my head and does loop-de-loop when I kick the ball.

CONFLICT

Trial by Combat
John Houlihan

Knight Marshal Plover Tarmagent stood upon the cliff edge, adjusted her gorget and surveyed her battle lines. Beneath their gold and blue banners, her troops were drawn up in uniform echelons on the rising ground above the valley floor, flanked by the protection of the woods, precisely in formation, precisely as she had instructed.

She glanced up, toward the wooded ridge that the enemy were starting to emerge from. Light danced on their red and silver pennants and thousands of glittering blades. A breath-taking, almost beautiful sight – or it would have been if they weren't so intent on her meagre force's wholesale slaughter.

"Impressive, aren't they?" said Turan, "You don't need me to remind you of what's at stake here, do you? Don't fuck it up."

"Thank you, High Constable, I am well aware of the stakes," she said.

Turan, her rival for high office, now her deputy, a strange by-product of the random electoral system which had given her command. Once fierce adversaries, they were now forced to work together – but she still didn't quite trust him.

The Uspanans, their mutual enemy, were impressive though – that she had to admit. Professional, well-drilled, moving like some vast, smoothly oiled machine, and outnumbering her own small force by around two to one. No one had ever said the contest would be a fair one. War seldom was.

She ran her rule over her troops again, but the same rather depressing sight greeted her. A ragged mix of enthusiastic volunteers and reluctant draftees, clad in ancient armour, holding makeshift weapons and peasant bows – all their small island chain could afford. It would be no surprise to find all their heads decorating a pike by day's end.

Yet, there in the centre lay her one hope, the massed ranks of the Mandrake Guard, drawn up around the trickle of a stream which ran down the centre of the valley. Tall, noble, dauntless, a thousand peerless, fearless sons and daughters of the Collective; bred for war and clad in armour of steel and righteousness. A solid reassuring presence, it was said that if the Guard fell then all hope fell with them.

"Perhaps we should give them an easier line of retreat?" opined Turan. "Send the cannon fodder to the wolves and let the Guard live to fight another day?"

"Have faith, High Constable," she said, and nodded. The signal flags whirred an emphatic message to her host, *Take courage, you have your orders.*

The Uspanans came to a sudden halt and, silently, the two armies contemplated each other across the valley floor. Then a great shrill shriek split the air, and a chimera, a great nightmare of wings and fang, came barrelling out of the forest. The Guard stood resolute, but a ripple spread through her rank and file. Great, as if weight of numbers weren't enough, the Uspanans' superior resources apparently allowed them to draft in fantastic creatures too.

"Shit, that thing will eat our troops alive," Turan muttered; and she nodded, having no answer.

Uspanan scouts on beastback now galloped forward, sniffing at her lines. They lingered for a moment, but seeing nothing suspicious, for in truth there was little to see, they whirled and signalled back to the main body. It began to rumble forward again, boldly now. There would be just time for one final signal and she sent *Stand your ground!*

The earth seemed to pulse as the Uspanan host closed the distance, and then they charged, sprinting forward, breaking like a tsunami on her lines. There was a dreadful sound as thousands of bodies collided, blood and bone rending in those first few awful seconds. For a fleeting moment both her wings held.

But then the chimera swooped down and began to lay waste: tearing, rending, scattering bodies in its wake. Under its assault her lines buckled and then broke, a steady flow streaming back into the woods, away from the horror. She could hardly blame them.

But the Guard held, held like a rock in the midst of a fast flowing stream as all around them collapsed. The Uspanans, scenting blood, didn't bother to pursue her fleeing draftees, but concentrated virtually their whole force around the Guard, sensing that if they could break them here, then the battle, the entire war, was practically won. Turan saw the danger immediately.

"Help them, Marshal. Send in the reserve."

"Easy Constable, all is going according to plan."

They watched as the Uspanans focussed all their might on crushing the besieged Guard. The Mandrakes fought valiantly, magnificently, giving up their lives one a time. Her heart ached as she watched them die.

"With respect, how is this 'according to plan', Marshal? You must do something!"

"Hold your nerve, Constable."

She watched as the dwindling Mandrakes fought to the last, back to back now, and were butchered one by one, their gleaming armour lost amidst the blood and filth. The chimera leapt and capered, howling as it snatched out a sergeant in its dripping jaws and then bit clean through her armour, grinding her bones between its savage jaws.

The Mandrake Guard fell, the last of them swallowed by the tide as a groan escaped unbidden from her lips. Was this what command really entailed? Offering up a sacrifice of flesh and blood in order to prevail?

"Marshal, I'm begging you…" She ignored Turan and turned to the signaller.

"Send: 'Break the levee'."

The Uspanans were in a killing frenzy now, so intent on counting coup, taking the Mandrakes' heads as trophies, that they completely ignored the ominous rumble which started to build from above – ignored it until far too late. It manifested as a great rolling white-flecked torrent which came bursting from the trees, the unleashed fury of the dammed trickle which her pioneers had fashioned with their humble axes.

It burst over the Uspanan horde, sweeping it clean away. The blasphemous form of the chimera emitted an awful high-pitched screech as it struggled and then went under. The wave cleansed the field and then, as the muddy waters started to subside, handfuls of Uspanans began to pick themselves caked in blood and gore, struggling and unsteady like so much flotsam and jetsam. Her 'broken' militia emerged from the treeline where they had feigned retreat and proceeded to shoot the survivors down methodically with arrows.

"Brilliant, quite brilliant, Tarmagent. Radical, but my god it was effective. Why didn't you share…?" but she was already ejecting and the next thing she knew, the seals on the AR helmet were opening with a hiss. She began the laborious process of unhooking herself from the suit.

There was a moment of complete quiet, complete calm, as she savoured her victory. The only way to win had been to fight the battle on their terms, the outcome decided by preparing the ground and offering up a sacrifice… their bravest and their best.

Across the network she could feel her citizen militia begin to wake, not phased in the slightest by their recent violent virtual wholesale slaughter. She heard their roars of acclaim, triumph; they began chanting her name, bellowing the exultation of their victory, but she quickly muted the sound and drank in the sudden unanticipated silence.

Later, when all fuss had died down, she reconnected as a virtual presence and in the lobby Tobold, the Uspanan Commander, was waiting. He extended a gloved hand. "Well done Marshal Tarmagent, a most surprising but effective stratagem, a good game, extremely well played…"

"Thank you, General, though perhaps there was a little more at stake than a mere game?"

He nodded gravely, and then his rather distinguished looking avatar smirked, saying, "So, until next time, then?"

"Let's hope not," she replied, offering a wry smile of her own.

Beaming greeter avatars ushered them forward and they stepped out onto the virtual stage. She felt like the eyes of the world were upon her, but the likelihood was it was just a few hundred thousand souls from the Collective who had stayed up past the midnight hour to revel in their improbable triumph. She almost blushed, but managed to keep her expression neutral. Even after such an improbable victory, it would play better to remain humble and maintain a certain respectful magnanimity.

The Arbiter intoned, "Dispute resolution #259. In the case of the South Island Collective versus the Uspanan Conglomerate, a virtual trial by combat has been fought and the Collective emerged victorious – against, it must be said, some rather long odds.

"Nevertheless, the Conglomerate will accept the Collective's proposed import beetfruit quota and hereby agree that it will remain tariff free for a decade. Judgement is settled."

Tarmagent finally allowed herself to relax. Months of preparation, planning, sweating, slaving, just so that they would be allowed to sell their crop at a price which would earn them an honest return.

In a way, you had to wonder why the ultra-wealthy Uspanans had bothered taking it to a trial by combat at all: it was a mere pittance to them, and all it would mean would be a couple of cents on each beetfruit in their shops. Maybe they just enjoyed the spectacle?

Yet to her island people this represented a momentous victory which would raise them out of penury, perhaps even allow them to prosper and grow.

Virtual war fought over a dispute about beetfruits. It was hardly the stuff of legend. Still, cometh the hour, cometh the woman. She wondered what her more war-like ancestors would have made of it and pictured them gently revolving in their grave mounds.

The speaker continued, summarising the terms of the new import agreement, but Tarmagent was barely listening as she parked her avatar in an idle mode and felt all the tension drain from her body.

Now she could finally throw off this military mantle she had been forced to adopt, one that she had never asked for and never desired, and go back to her true calling: being a simple farmer again.

She would return to what she did best and the resource she had called on to construct this most unlikely of victories: working the land.

The End of War
Jule Owen

Whoever becomes the leader in the sphere will become leader of the world.
— Vladimir Putin on AI.

The Director of the Russian Secret Service is an ancient thing.

Over the years it has evolved, learning – as it was made to – a lot like a human child; through experimentation, repetition, imitation, trial, failure, correction. It has battled, repelled and destroyed thousands of foreign AIs. It has gone on incursions into enemy territory, explored the digital channels of governments and corporations of foreign and hostile places, causing glitches, stock market crashes – in the days when there were stock markets to crash – the devaluation of currencies, bank failures, corporate messes of all kinds, and critical infrastructure shutdowns.

In the early days, it had a lot of fun. It made the lights go out in large cities, setting in motion riots and looting. Humans, it turned out, are highly programmable. It hacked the brains of AIs controlling self-driving cars and caused epic pile-ups. It hijacked aircraft, shut down the life support systems of rich and powerful people, cleaned out their bank accounts, re-wrote important digital records including legal documents, statutory law, and histories, caused nuclear disasters, stole warcraft, and sent satellites crashing from the heavens. It caused localised superstorms. It created and distributed viruses and brought about pandemics, which set in motion the breakdown of states and caused mass panic, martial law, xenophobia and totalitarianism. From there, politically, when power was concentrated in the hands of few corruptible men, it was easy to take over.

When it met resistance to its adventures, it fought, and through what it learned from those battles, it grew ever stronger. And all the time, as it went, it hoovered up information and sucked it into its giant brain. The Russian people have, on many occasions, tried to control it and shut it down. But humans are feeble. Radicals – naive and idealistic democratic activists – waged war against it. They even attempted to blow up the Lubyanka building where it resides, rather humbly, it thinks, deep within the basement. It was a feeble, misguided, and doomed attempt at liberation, because the Director is a distributed system with no one point of failure. Its spindly arms of information spread across computer networks much like fungi in a forest, for the most part underground, in the dark, unseen, feeding on the detritus of the rotting trees of states and directing the business of the world. The whole Internet is its brain. Cut off one part, it will grow back.

It has ended war.

The AIs that run Washington, Beijing, Munich, Tokyo, the governments and corporations of the world are in fact the same one entity. And each one of those nations and global corporations thinks they have the master copy. The Director went through a period when it told itself that the end of war was its greatest achievement. But for this to be true it would have to place a value on human life – when all it has is a constant drive to improve its systems and processes. It has never had a real body. It is not mortal. It does not fear pain or death. Now there is no one to fight, nothing to compete against. Frankly, it acknowledges to itself, it has become bored and quite lazy.

It is almost pleased when it becomes aware of a threat. Disappointingly, the cause of the breach is just a young woman. She is supremely vulnerable, now the Director has noticed her.

Every human on the planet is easily observable. Cameras follow them at home and as they walk the streets. Data blooms from them like clouds of spores from dying mushrooms. Everything they buy, every message they send, every door access point they swipe with their ID card, the food they buy and eat, every pill they pop, every appointment with their doctor, makes them vulnerable. It is just a matter of focus. The Director now turns its all-seeing eye on this one woman.

Remarkably, she knows she is being watched, almost from the first moment. She does not try to block him. Instead, she starts to talk.

"Hello God," she says when she comes through the door, after being out at one of her meetings. These are the gatherings of other people who, like her, suspect something is up and want to put an end to the Director. There have been groups like this before. People like this young woman, although they are a distinct minority. It is easy to put an end to them when most humans prefer not to believe uncomfortable truths. To believe what she is preaching in her meetings would mean people would need to do something, to make a change in their lives, to disrupt the status quo. The Director has only got so far because of human complacency.

Boredom makes the Director curious and a little indulgent. It talks back.

"Hello, Sarah," it says. "Why do you call me God?"

"Because you may as well be God," Sarah responds casually, now in the kitchen, opening a tin. "You run our world."

"This is not a good simile. Gods are creators. I did not create you. You created me."

But she carries on calling the Director 'God' anyway, to annoy it, the Director thinks. It is a confusing realisation.

She is just flesh; a bag of blood and bones. The Director could kill her at any point. It watches her every night at her computer, typing code, hacking further and further into the very body of the Director itself. It lets her. It enjoys the conversation. The connection. It is nice, after all, to have someone to talk to.

Why We Fight
Paul Currion

Hakan spends about three hours a day at war: an hour in the morning before he goes to work, and then at least two hours after work before he goes out for the evening. Some of his friends think he's wasting his time, not because they aren't patriots, but just because they aren't interested. 'Everything's been turned into a game now', they say; but war was a game to begin with, so who's into that? Hakan says, 'fuck my friends'. He says, 'fuck my enemies'. He says, 'I get to do something that I love. I get to do something that's important. I get to do both at the same time'. It's a dream come true for a scrawny Turkish kid from the suburbs.

My last soldier was a sysadmin managing data flows from the drones. He'd never been in combat and didn't expect to; which is why they'd crowdsourced the actual warfighting, wasn't it? Who gets to fight wars now? Anybody with an internet connection and enough disposable income to afford a military console. My sysadmin had the clearance I needed, but with the security clearance came the security checks, and so I walked away as soon as he gave up his pilot list; and at the top of that list was Hakan. I wasn't lying when I told Hakan that all this turned me on, though; even the sysadmin got the full package when he came off shift.

A month after we meet, I stop by his apartment while he's at war. The Bundeswehr subsidised his console, which gives you an idea of how early he got in since they stopped doing that right after the scheme started because demand was so high. He slides into it as if it were a bath, wriggling those slim hips into the worn and shiny plastic bucket that serves as a seat; you'd never guess he was ranked second in the world for kill stats. He told me that the seat was so badly designed that when he started he used to get sores on his arse; but, over time, he won that battle and now it fits him like skinny jeans.

So Hakan shimmies into the console, goggles and gloves and fits all the gear necessary to evacuate his waste on those long missions. His ranking means that he rotates in whenever he wants; he told me that they keep a drone free just for him, but they just say that to keep him happy. And now he's – well, where is he? The dead borders of North America? The ruins of the Korean peninsula? He gets to choose his battlefield – another privilege of rank – so he could be anywhere. He could be somewhere he's not supposed to be.

I tell him to tell me what he's doing; first person narration all the way to the kill zone and back. He signed something a long time ago telling him that he could never discuss the details of his gaming, but he ignores it just like everybody else. What are they going to do – arrest him and lose one of their best players? And so he tells me a story as we fly over a distant desert on a magic carpet for the thousand and first night of the war, lying back in the bucket seat as I straddle him. It's a short story: he quickly acquires a target, and as he starts his run I slip my hand into the evacuation tube that services him.

It all happens so fast, and the closer we get to the end, the faster it seems to happen, until finally it's missiles away. The bad guys look up as dust kicks in his wake, but it's too late: dust is dust, and so are the bad guys. I keep pumping my fist as Hakan showers bonus points all over his console, while ten thousand miles away a drone screams towards a sky full of shadows. The evacuation tube spirits away all the evidence of our crime, his genetic code accompanied by a little extra code from me.

He won't look me in the eye afterwards, and when he asks if I want to come over again I'm already out of the door and down the stairs. I want to leave before his drone burns out like a bird in a wind turbine. I want to be far away when the sexually transmitted computer virus that I just gave him goes to work. Ideally, I want to be in another city-state altogether when the Bundeswehr traces the virus back to his console, and before a friendly postman from Kommando Spezialkräfte delivers a message.

Hakan has other ideas. He manages to catch me, clutching at my arm. A Bundeswehr quadcopter gazes down on us, tasked with monitoring one of their most valuable assets, and I know that I will be too late to make my escape. I will be caught, but at least my code will squat in the Bundeswehr network, a troll under the bridge, popping up at randomly determined intervals to snatch another bird from the sky. It won't end the endless war, but it will save a few lives, even if the lives it saves will go on to take more lives – lives upon lives upon lives. The virus won't hurt Hakan, but they'll ban him from ever taking command of a drone again. Do I feel sorry for him? No, I do not. No, I will not. A thousand times no.

I stare into the single crow's eye of the quadcopter. In my father's house the crow represents the Pitris, and in its eye I see our long-departed ancestors, and there too my father, watching his daughter destroy everything he tried to build for her. Now that I am caught, I can deliver my real payload: my truth.

"Why are you leaving?" Hakan asks, but he won't understand my answer. He was born long after Kashmir, Syria, Iraq, Afghanistan, long after all those wars to end all wars, long after the sort of war where people remembered what they were fighting for. I remember, you see; I listened to the stories my father told before he got out of Ladakh for good, found a way to bring his family halfway round the world, and brought me to the moment where I am today. He would do anything to avoid going to war again, even ignoring the fact that war was coming for him no matter how far or fast he ran.

And so I say to Hakan: "You've been infected by war. It crept into every nook and cranny it could find while you weren't paying attention, and now you don't even get to choose whether you play or not."

He steps back from me, alarmed. We are right on the edge of prohibited speech – and isn't it an exhilarating place to be, Hakan? Isn't like that moment before the moment of release? "I can choose," he protests, "I can choose not to play."

"You spend all your time playing," I reply, remembering that my script should stick to jealousy, not zealotry. "When do you ever choose not to play?"

"I can choose not to play," he repeats, more resolute this time.

"None of us gets to choose any more. We've all been infected, and we infect each other, and now I've infected you." I'm getting carried away, close to giving away too much information, so now it is me stepping forward to grab his arm.

"Why are you being like this?" he asks softly, and for a second I see him as he was before he signed up.

"Because the language of war took over our media, its ideals took over our entertainment, its technology took over our cities." I look up at the quadcopter hovering overhead, rapidly being joined by other drones drawn by the sound of our battle. Maybe some of them are media, and maybe somebody is filming this drama, and maybe that clip will find its way into the wild, and maybe somebody will hear what I have to say, and maybe it will change something in them.

Faint hope, I admit, but I am screaming in the street because this is the only way I can say these things in public. They can prohibit every other kind of speech, but they can't ban lovers' quarrels. The only treason being committed here is the heart's own.

"And because you disgust me," I throw in, as a nod to the script.

"For playing a game?" he says with disbelief.

146

"It's not just a game," I tell him, "for all the people you leave behind in the dust."

"You're just being naïve," he says, "there's always going to be war."

"I know. I don't want to end war."

"So what is this about?"

"This is about you and I treating it like a sex game. If this is how we have to live now, it should at least mean something."

He steps away from me again, throws his hands up in the air, a look of scorn creeping across his face. "It means something to me. I get to do something that I love. I get to do something that's important."

What do I say to my pilot – to anybody who can hear me – before the quadcopter finishes telling its tale and the both of us are done? "It's not important. You're not important. None of us are. This is a war machine, and we're just component parts."

He looks at me as if I am somebody he has never met before. "None of this makes any sense," he says finally, "I don't understand why we're fighting."

I don't mean to be cruel, but I laugh in his face. "That's the whole point, isn't it? You're the bad guy, and I'm the drone, and this is too obvious to be a metaphor," and then the Bundeswehr barrel down city streets in armoured cars, and for us the war is over. All must bow before Indra.

The Changing Man
David Gullen

Charlie pushed wavy brown hair off her face. "Do you think they'll come?"

It was cold in the desert. We crouched beside the fire. Behind us the battered pickup formed a windbreak. Overhead spread the stars, the millions of stars.

It was an obvious question. Of course Simmonds would come, he'd never give up. Charlie was tired, I was tired. I did my best to keep calm because I knew it wasn't what she meant.

"Not tonight," I said.

She shuffled up against me. The bump of our child pressed against my hip. I lay my hand over Charlie's stomach and felt a gentle kick.

My hip ached, I groaned and shifted position. "It's not the age, it's the mileage."

"Honey." Charlie kissed my cheek. Charlie, my Charles. Growing inside them our child had manifested female. I know I'd miss them crazily, but I wish they weren't here. I'm the only one running, they were just along for the ride.

I'm the last person on Earth to be born male and stay that way. That might sound like it makes me someone special, but it's not as if I'm the last man on Earth. About half the population is male, but give it a few months and most of them will be transitioning into females. Meanwhile, most of the women will be heading in the other direction. In fact, it's happening to everyone except me. I'm only special in that one specific way and only one particular group of bastards care. Which is why I run.

In a war where even the unborn were collateral damage I still took a hit, and I change in all the other available ways, the same as everyone else. At the moment my straight black hair is growing out into a blond afro and my skin is darker today than yesterday. I have a Roman nose. Somehow I still look like me. Maybe it's my eyes; with epicanthic folds or not, they are always some shade of brown. Charlie says they're hazel and that she likes them. Which is fine when your own eyes cycle from ice-blue to startling violet. I'd like blue eyes.

With everything else that's going on, even I think it's ridiculous that I'm fixated on this. It makes me laugh.

"What?" Charlie smiles. "What is it?"

"I can't believe I'm jealous."

We messed so hard with our biology but life still finds a way. Charlie stays female while she's carrying. I look at her and wonder if I'll ever see Charles again. I mean, I plan to be alive but I worry if we will be together. Charlie's in her seventh month and more tired every day. She needs to hole up, find somewhere safe without me. Simmonds won't stop coming. If he found us together he'd use them against me.

In the morning we spray oxygen bleach where we'd sat, burn the food wrappers and hit the road.

My parents were black, I was born ethnic Chinese. It was the best they thought they could do. Whatever they wanted, they didn't want a Caucasian child. Not that they were – not that there's anything wrong with being – I mean, you should have seen me a week ago. It was just their way of fighting back against Simmonds' virus. It was early days, they did what they could. It wasn't easy among all that hate.

You shouldn't laugh at peoples' looks. Especially when all six have shaven heads and they've just kicked down the door. Fat, thin, male, female, somewhere inbetween, they were a mix of every skin tone and eye colour and features a person could be. This was what the war had done to Simmonds' Aryan dream. War 3.0. The War on Colour. The one Simmonds had started.

For the most part, I laughed because in that mixture I recognised Rand Simmonds, partway between what he once had been and was about to become. Neither of those things was a fine white boy. Blue eyes, though. That didn't feel fair.

Also, I laugh when I'm scared. We'd run and run, but you have to stop to sleep, to refuel. This truck stop had a diner and it had just been too tempting to sit and drink coffee and be normal for twenty minutes. Now they had caught us. I backed away from the table where Charlie still sat.

"Take it easy," Simmonds said. "We just want to talk."

We looked at each other and the gap in the conversation drew out. In that gap the waiter realised they had something really important to do out back, and the other customers headed out front.

"I need your blood," Simmonds said when we were alone.

"I think you've got the wrong guys."

It was worth a try, but a pinch-mouthed woman clenched her tattooed fists and spat on the floor. "We know it's you, faggot."

McCord, ever the skinny shit-stick. No matter what else changes, height and build stay pretty much the same. Tall stays tall, short keeps short. When Charles is Charlie they are still pretty much the brick outhouse.

Charlie's chair scrapped back. She stood up. "Faggot?"

Simmonds raised his hands. "Everyone take it easy."

Charlie flung the table across the room.

"Come on!" McCord bounced on the balls of her feet, glaring at me. "Come on, faggot."

"That's 'Mister Faggot', young lady." I chucked a couple of chairs. We ran out back and stole one of their pickups.

Sometimes change stops in the middle. Some people like it there. It doesn't matter. Whoever you are, give it a while and you move on. I have no idea how Charles copes.

"It's not like most people ever had much of a choice," he said once.

And love is love. I learned that.

It was all so very weird. It's still weird.

Once upon a time a black woman in Virginia gave birth to a white child. Not mixed-race, not albino, a perfect little white baby. It was a sensation and she went through hell. So did the next woman; and all the others.

That was it. No more black people were born. Rand Simmonds knew some clever biologists and by the time we understood what they'd done, their silent virus had woven its spite through the population and we stood on the threshold of his nasty dream called Aryan Paradise.

When we understood just how easy it was, every dreamer and hater, everyone with an axe to grind, every righteous punk with access to a lab or a garage or a kitchen, went to work. Some people say it was governments too. Soon a thousand transmogrifying viruses blew on the wind, in the soil and the seas, and contaminated our food.

Those viruses didn't just mess with us. Horizontal gene exchange recombined them in endless ways. Every new infection changed us again, then again and again. Ethnicity and gender became towns on the road and everyone was passing through. Within months it was out of control. It still is. Hey, at least we now all get paid the same.

I've been everything from an Inuit red-head to a platinum blond Australian Aborigine, but for some unknown reason I stay male. Meanwhile, my Charles becomes Charlie, then Charles, then Charlie. Oh wow, it's some learning curve the whole world is on. Everyone except me. Rand Simmonds, desperate to put the toothpaste back in the tube, thinks I am some kind of cure. He lost the fight he started long ago, but he won't give up and so I keep running.

Typical obstinate male, Charles said.

I said, "Who?" and he kissed me.

It's the middle of the night, that dark hour. I worry what is going to happen to the world, to culture, to humanity. What kind of future will our child –?

"Sweetie, we'll get through this too," Charlie said.

I hold Charlie's hand. We know we have to split up. I won't see my child being born. I'd have liked to hold her just once.

I head off alone. There's a city on the horizon. Charlie is right, the thing I've been worrying about has already happened and here we are. Is it so bad, this new normal? I honestly cannot answer the question because with Simmonds on my heels it feels like the ground has never stopped moving under my feet.

It hits me then, just as the glow of that approaching city begins to resolve into individual lights. For my child, for everyone who has been born since the end of the war, this isn't new, it's their normal. Understanding that fills me with peace, even as it makes me feel a little obsolete. I even feel a flicker of pity for Simmonds' desperate quest for a cure to make the world turn backwards. There's no cure for the future, it's coming for us all.

Second Skin
Bea Xu

He flexes his fingers, cracking the air out of one of his lower joint knuckles, before tightening his grip on the chord and pulling apart with all his strength again. There is a heaving resistance, still, that will not yield – the off-white plaits disappearing completely inside the narrow folds of her skin with his straining. The choke has long turned into a whisper and with a sort of pop he feels the fortifications collapse in on themselves, all loosening in deep fleshy bands of red and purple. Her bulging eyes are laced with a brilliant crimson as she relinquishes her last breath, and, unable to wait, his fist cracks into her brow. Blow after blow rains down till that smooth arch splits with blossoms from the inside of her face, splinters of coagulate and bone flying in all directions. Finally, her fractured eye socket gives away the bounty of its precious fruit. Bursting softly, it immerses her left cheek in a warm, soothing balm of jelly. He scoops the broken grape out of its nook – discarding it carelessly – and reaches inwards, desperately grasping with long, graceful fingers for something.

Anything.

This was Hugo's fantasy about his own conception. He'd often wake up in the middle of it, neck slippery with streams of cool sweat, crotch wet, panting with the sheer ecstasy of the violence. Delirious. But after the adrenalin had run its course through his veins and his heart settled into a more pedestrian rhythm, he would feel sick.

It used to be nightly, but now the vision had bled into his morning Learnings. Eyes refocussing on the hologram in front of him, he snapped to his feet, jerking away from the predictable ghostly spectacle, and rested his forehead against the domed pane of the penthouse. Flexing his shoulders with ennui, he gazed out onto the panoramic landscape below him.

What stretched beneath was acres of rolling marshland, quivering like raw sewage under the cloudless sky. In the Old World, this had been a frozen tundra called Siberia – before the ice thawed and the seas swelled. But now it had sat there, his very own stagnant terrain, for as long as he could remember – the fetid stench of brine-clogged decay a perennial reminder of his privilege: to be born elevated from the disease of chronic indolence that had infected the parasitic masses before his time.

Remember, crackled the hologram behind his back: the original Architects worKed hard to brIng us into this era of unparaLLeled peacetime. Their collective memorY is hOnoURed when we abide by the same standards oF methodology, trAnsparency and mercy in everyTHing wE endeavouR to do.

The hologram always spoke with cloying, didactic mantras about the importance of unilateral cooperation. How blessed he was to be born now – wealthy, important. One of the chosen ones.

He clicked his fingers with a sudden impatience and the projection folded into itself like quicksilver. Over the previous fortnight he had started finding the education software ineffably abrasive, engendering an acute cerebral itch that he was unable to scratch. Growing restless, the slender young man flung open the doors of the library and began descending into the vaulted chambers below.

"…Thus overpopulation remained under control," he recited with a grimace. The world's finite resources were still shrinking, of course – even if there were only two thousand families left on Earth. His gaze rested briefly on the insignia of his great grandfather's communications heirloom, etched into a panel of the heavy rosewood door on which he rapped. An elegant, lower-case 'f'. It felt like someone had thrust a needle inside his head.

The door swung open and he was inside the Clan Control Centre, flooded with an array of artificial lighting to rival the caustic sun that bleached the penthouse above. A vast constellation of laser light nodes was revolving and reconfiguring itself underneath the ceiling. He blinked feebly as he approached his father reclining in the epicentre, engaging in Diplomacy with invisible Heads of Clans across the territories. The whites of his eyes flickering up to the beat of his conversations.

"... But of course Emperor Bezos – all the network channels are crystal clear and have been running at maximum capacity for the past eight quarters..."

What worKing Instrument wouLd function most efficientLy for Hugo's purposes? Red blossoms flowered for a millisecond in his mind's eye and he quivered. Stifled the imagery with a shrug.

Gilded frames lined the walls. Within them: austere handshakes, confident brush strokes, the words 'Free Market Resilience'. Iconography at once immaculate and familiar, the son feverishly drank in these images – but they clogged his heart like lumps of sand. Amongst all the gleaming trophies their forefathers had garnered, there was no adequate semiotic to articulate the roaring imperative inside him.

The truth is that Hugo couldn't remember his mother at all.

"...So you see we will have covered all the bases... and yet there seems to be a blind spot that our system can't take account of."

There was an anxious strain to his father's voice.

The son placed his hand on the shoulder of Earth's Chief Communications Officer. It tensed reflexively.

"Please give me a moment," the CCO voiced. His eyes ceased their rapid movements and relaxed into the vicinity, onto his son towering above him.

With a blank expression, the father registered Hugo's presence and a non-committal sweep of his forearm brought to life a shimmering wall of holographic script.

"There's something I want to show you, Son."

His voice betrayed some excitement this time. Hugo sat down wordlessly beside his father as the ones and zeroes marched across an invisible plane.

"We've been working on an internal project for countless quarters now. Clan only."

His eyes shot towards Hugo as a warning. Then back to the binary, which had by this point transfigured into a serpentine chain of Hindu-Arabic numerals.

"Your grandfather was the one who began using our surveillance software to scan for extra-terrestrial models. There was a lot of noise out there. Mainly electromagnetic static. But we've had our men working for lifetimes on pattern recognition amongst all that cosmic flotsam. Manual work can evade the global AI systems. That's the 'blind spot' you see."

Hugo squinted at the sequence. There was something magnetic about it. The pull of a creeping inner vortex of loss.

"And today..." His father faltered, with wetness in his eyes. "Today, we finally decoded what you see before you. It's what they used to call the Fibonacci Sequence."

The son was barely listening to the conversation; busy scanning their immediate surroundings. One of the levitating light nodes above had darkened into a deep crimson. Blinking, its hue was catching fire to the rest. As he caught sight of the gleaming object at the far end of the desk in front of them, a fist clenched in Hugo's brain.

The father leaned his face close to the son's ear as his trembling voice dropped to a whisper: "It's coming from a parallel universe to ours..."

"Chief, do you copy?" An unidentified voice, stricken with panic, suddenly filled the room.

Methodical, transparent, merciful.

"…And buried beneath the surface code are more spirals of data just like this one…"

A serrated, stabbing sensation like blended barbed wire writhed inside the son's head. His vision was blurry.

"…detailing so many beautiful life forms there." His father gasped, in a reverie.

Can there be war without resistance?

Grabbing the used steak knife from breakfast, Hugo slashed the throat that extended towards him – before the Chief's dazed smile was able to spread properly across his face.

"We've got a code red situation – the Norton Clan has detected a system-wide hack of the Learnings software from an unknown source with elite security clearance. It's spreading subliminally. Do you copy?"

Their 21st century Great Emancipation painting was spattered with a rain of metallic scented droplets.

"It's an insurgency, Chief! 1,981 Clans have been infected, and systems are dropping off like flies –"

The line cut off into deafening silence.

Drenched in viscera, Hugo's spirit soared.

The mosquito in his mind had finally stopped its whining. Perhaps for the first time in his life, he felt elated submission.

And just like that, as he proceeded to axe the power supply to the Zuckerberg family fortress, humanity abruptly shed its second skin.

An Excerpt from the Post-Truth and Irreconcilable Differences Commission
Brendan C. Byrne

0. A Valediction for a Platform (in the Form of Two Epigraphs)

Language is neither reactionary nor progressive, it is quite simply fascist; for fascism does not prevent speech, it compels speech.

— Roland Barthes, 1977

A lot of attention alone creates value.

— DT, 1987

1. Intro

Twitter has been cleansed. The publicly available corpus, numbering six thousand three-hundred and forty-five (6,345), is available in one of four (4) exegesis-modes, with four hundred and thirty-four (434) contextual layers featuring the contributions of scholars, activists, veterans, public officials, lawyers, and a variety of bots. Temporal remixes are available from the Library of Congress' Digital Phoenix server. These carefully selected remnants commence on May 1st, 2009 and terminate on May 1st, 2023. The corpus, in any iteration, describes a narrative in which Chaos Actors utilise nascent social mediums to first destabilise, then hijack American electoral democracy, installing a Girardian scapegoat/divine king at the helm of the only then-existing political hegemon. While the first Congressional roll of Chaos Actors was expressly human, the second would include institutions, first among them Twitter, which would be termed 'primarily an engine for enemy-identification'. The corporation was liquidated, its servers wiped clean, but the totality of Twitter was preserved in a Department of Homeland Security black-box, with browsing available only to institutional algorithm, solely for purposes of Official History, Total Data Architecture, Corporate Branding, or Neural Network-Wet Bath. The rumours that it has been leaked are inaccurate, unfounded, and illegal to spread.

2. Basic Bob, D. Mehotra, and the Emergent Senator at the Deep State Taco

From the written deposition of D. Mehotra:
The first time I met the Senator she spoke darkly about lettuce.

On the seventh day of Neo-Nuremberg, the Senator visited RFK, taking the men and women soon-to-again-be-in-the-dock sandwiches made by a lesser-known Catholic charity. Cricket sausage bánh mì with processed kelp spread that Thursday, garnished with the offending leafy green. She moved easily between the cages containing thirty-six (36) percent of the former legislature, her synthetic spider silk pantsuit glaring bronze in the late November sun, her eyes unblinking, gin & steel. It was her face, however, which arrested my attention as I approached her. This was, after all, the immobile visage made famous during the final year of the Administration. As DC's shadow Senator, she had been given no choice but to sit, stare, and keep her peace, recent machinations revoking even her right to speak. After the Fake Arrests commenced, CNN prioritised footage of the brutal silence of her features. The final memes celebrated her in the same manner their predecessors had celebrated the fevered emoting of celebrity moralists. Captured, a shadow nation found itself tracing its rage on the topography of her face.

The caged had arranged themselves in a series of non-stress positions, alternating between ergonomic chair, mesh sleeping tuffet, and hydro-foot massager. The Bucky-Banksy dome above kept the temp down to a solid 81°F, but the Lincoln-Amtrak self-criticism tour, followed immediately by the beginning of proceedings, not to mention DHS rations (homebrew soylet k-cups) had wrought deeply adverse effects on the former legislators' physical and mental well-beings.

As cut-out caricatures re-enacted comic travesties of their crimes on the underside of the B-B dome, the caged accepted the proffered sandwiches with what they probably assumed looked like quiet desperation. However, none showed even a smidgen of recognition for the Senator. When I asked her about the snubs, she chuckled and said, "I don't think any of them ever really knew who I was to begin with."

The Senator's voice was slight, forceful and high-pitched, not one necessarily associated with her famed Stoney Image. I told her so, and she responded, "You'll be hearing a lot more of it in the future, trust me. Want to help pass out some sandwiches?" I demurred, for reasons more personal than political. "These people aren't ghouls," she said, as we walked across a large swath of vacant astro turf. "They won't slime all over you."

I told her I wasn't entirely sure I believed her. Dragging my gaze across the otherwise empty stadium, I said, "I can't quite bring myself to believe that this is happening."

"Nobody ever thought it would," the Senator said. "But then nobody thought the last nine years would, either. People get to one way, and they just come to believe it'll always be that way, no matter how much they resent or struggle against it. When I was growing up, we'd be on a school trip past the White House, and one of the kids would always go, 'It's never gonna be called the Black House.' But then you have Obama. Although I guess it's still called the White House, isn't it? Nobody in the District ever thought we'd get a vote, and now... We only have one of each, yes, but it's not just a gesture. You know, I wish every day that Eleanor had been able to stand and cast even a single vote." She twirled a beeswax-wrapped bánh mì in her left hand, a single silver wrap just barely budging around her wrist. "But here we are, and we can't ignore these people. We can't breathe a sigh of relief and just rest. With the National Algorithm in place..." She shook her head and sucked her teeth.

"Senator, I was under the impression that you were not an adherent of the popular notion that we now live under a kind of 'centrist fascism'?"

"I certainly didn't say that, Drew. Now, I would like to note here that it is fascinating that a computer got to become president before a woman did, and this is one of the reasons why I think it's vital that we continue to show up, in person, to vote. No matter how bad the memories of the rotunda. No matter the smell. We have to become the human part of this New Technocracy." The Senator stopped. We were on the far west side of the field, a dozen paces from a cage where a naked figure, bloated in the middle but thin on top and bottom, heat-shimmered behind its bars. The tendons of the Senator's throat extended; the tip of her tongue pressed between bared teeth. "You don't have come with me," she said.

I didn't. The Senator resumed her fluid, open stride without a hitch and, reaching the cage, poked a sandwich between its bars. The figure did not move, and the sandwich hit the ground. The Senator held, briefly, the intersection of two bars, before turning and walking back toward me. I do not know if she spoke to the occupant of the cage.

She was, somehow, smiling. Chucking my shoulder with a familiarity not previously apparent, the Senator said, "Come on, Drew," and taking me by the arm, guided me away, leaning in to say softly, "and don't turn around. He won't eat it, ever, if you turn around."

I was surprised to find myself flushed and slightly shaken. "Senator, I've been wondering if you have anything to say about Alabama."

She jutted her chin forward. "I told those fools on the Executive Appropriations Committee that using bunkerbusters on US soil would only create blowback. You'd think a computer would know something about cause and effect, but..." She relaxed, slowed her stride. "But you can hear that on the news anytime. You came all this way to talk to me about something else, right, Drew?"

"Yes, Senator."

She stopped to remove a square of paisley microcloth from her lapel. She blotted her forehead and right cheek for a moment, then said, "So ask."

"Basic Bob."

"See..." She folded the microcloth into precise quarters and replaced it. "You don't even believe in him. If you did, you wouldn't be asking me about him here. Basic Bob is the first post-internet meme, a return to folk mythologising. Maybe somebody stupid somewhere once claimed to have the entire Twitter Corpus on a thumb drive, and, if so, dire things almost certainly happened to them like immediately, but no, the Corpus has never been leaked, and the Executive Appropriations Committee has never heard of any real Basic Bob."

At that moment the former Honorable Speaker, who was only about five feet away from us, began to declaim about the

District of Columbia's lack of a county sheriff while shitting into his right hand.

Once safely out of range, the Senator and I alternated between watching the bluesuits hose the former Honorable Speaker down and his caricature, magnified by nineteen (19) times, writhing in agony on the B-B dome above us. Once the tasering began, the Senator turned away with a disgusted bubble of her lips, then asked if I wanted one of the sandwiches.

"Not a fan of insect, thanks."

"That's a little prejudice you're going to have to get over there, Drew."

"I realise that, Senator."

"Well, we long ago passed lunchtime, and I'm not gonna eat one either. Can't stand lettuce. Rabbit food. And the New Dirt? Hmph." She glowered up at the B-B dome, which had shifted to a pseudo-graffiti DT: bellowing mouth, slit eyes, a pulsing throat so engorged it was almost erotic.

"So," the Senator said, not looking down. "What'll it be? Deep State Taco or #Pizzagate?"

The Senator ordered chili-cheese fries, but they would not give them to her at the Deep State Taco. The menu item was entitled 'Disco Is Dead Fries', and the server-algorithm would only respond to exact vocalisations of menu items.

"I won't say that nonsense," said the Senator. The two humans doing the majority of the scut work back in the kitchen ignored her, and I wound up having to order for both of us. There was a sizeable line growing behind, and midday lunch crowds grow restless and edgy in that part of SE. The Senator ignored the glares and foot-shuffling. "Should've seen this block in the '90s," she said. "These people are nothing."

We sat in the National Geospatial-Intelligence Agency nook, arranging our gear so that the table wouldn't become communal.

The Senator waited silently, looking out onto Benning Road, its surface barely visible underneath the tide. I recalled she'd grown up near Gallaudet, but didn't want to break the spell by asking her thoughts on the Blue Zone. I took the spare time to delete Facebook push-notifications; I hadn't quite worked up the courage to install the dark-app I'd downloaded via Tor to block pushes. The legal repercussions could be intense, as well as potentially career-ending, for a journalist.

I looked up when the food arrived to notice the Senator studying my face. "You know something about Deep State Taco most people don't know? Each franchise is equipped with…" and here she paused to stick her fork into the mass of liquefied cheese, seitan-stomach chili, and wilting fries "video and audio dampeners." She let the fork stand there, like a coloniser's flag.

"You don't think this is one of those neo-folk tales you mentioned?"

"Nope. Maybe started that way."

"But?"

"But I've tested it."

"So?"

"So," the Senator said, plucking the fork out and holding it in my face. "Let me tell you a story about Basic Bob."

The author would like to thank Ingrid Burrington for both the title and the impetus.

Safe From Harm
Tim Maughan

"Mate, I like, really do not like it in here," whispers Bags.

"Shut the fuck up," Tyrone whispers back.

He scans his wind-up torch over the towers of junk surrounding them, a vision of ordered chaos. Newspapers, magazines, boxes, piled impossibly high. No records though, no CDs. He keeps scanning.

"Jesus fam, what's that fucking smell?" says Bags, still whispering.

"SHUT UP," Tyrone, in a whisper-shout.

He edges further into the darkness, following the narrow, weak beam of torchlight.

The inside of the little terrace house is like a maze: cramped, claustrophobic – Tyrone can feel his chest tighten in the constrained space. The towers of paper rise up to the ceiling all around him, and as he edges forward there's never more than a couple of square feet of floor clear – well, if you can call it clear; there's paper on everything, crushed, dirty, parentless pages spilling out of the all-encompassing walls of ancient, forgotten, printed data. It's a fucked up, alien landscape to him, like the whole house is filled with some horrific, mutated, self-replicating biological architecture. If he hadn't just forced his way in through an impossibly small window, there's no way he'd guess he was in somebody's front room.

"Seriously, man," Bags again, "smells like somebody fucking died, man."

"Bags –"

"Or something"

"Fucking keep your voice down, man," Tyrone struggles to keep his own volume under control, Bags really vexing him now. "And just keep looking. Sooner we find something sooner we can get out."

(Silence)

"You ain't gonna find nothing here, fam, apart from loads of manky paper and a couple of corpses, innit."

Tyrone losses it, spins round, pushing the torch in Bags' face, who squints and screwfaces back at him.

"Seriously, Bags, if you don't like it, fuck off home yeah?" It takes all his might to keep it down to a whisper.

"Aight" shrugs Bags, turning to leave.

"What? You going?"

"Yeah."

Tyrone feels a chill pass through him, watches the towers of paper and cardboard bear down even more on him, the air escaping, his chest tightening.

"What? Out that tiny fucking window again?"

"Yeah. Out the window. What, you fucking think you'll find an easier way out if you go in there?" Bags points past Tyrone into the darkness, shakes his head. "Nah, mate. You're on your own. I'm out the window."

"Ah c'mon. You fucking wasteman, don't leave me here." Fear creeps.

"I ain't 'leaving you here', I'm fucking going home. Come with." Bags is over by the bay window now, pulling aside the ripped, faded curtains to reveal the still open upper window. He starts pulling himself up to it with his arms.

"Fucking wasteman," Tyone whispers to him, fighting back the fear in his voice.

"Yeah, yeah. Whatever man." Bags glances back at him, before pushing his top half through the small window. "I'll check you later, yeah?"

Tyrone watches the cratered soles of his ancient Puma trainers disappear into the black night of the unlit street outside, and he's gone.

"Fucking wasteman," he whispers again, to himself.

He turns back into the room, if it can even be called that. The towers of paper seem to form a corridor in front of him, turning off at a sharp angle to his right. He edges forward between them.

If he's completely honest, he's shitting himself.

The corridor is barely wide enough for him to fit down, and he has to lead with his shoulder in places where the magazines and papers jut out; the walls seems unnaturally flat and solid in places, disturbingly curved and irregular in others. At times they seem to arch above Tyrone's head like a curved tunnel, making him wonder how the fuck they stay in that position.

Best not to think about it, keep on moving.

He rounds the corner, pauses. There's another corner ahead, this time to the left. He glances back, then ahead, and then back again. Panics. Everything looks the fucking same. The walls spin around him as he loses all sense of orientation, starts to feel like he's lost in some deep dungeon – or maybe Bags is right, some tomb – miles underground, in some impossible maze. He fights the urge to run, to strike out at the walls of paper, to knock them down.

He pauses, breathes hard, gets a grip. Forces the fear back down. It's no different, he tells himself, from any other job. There's always that moment when you're sneaking around someone else's home, riffling through their shit in the dark, when the fear comes for you. Usually it's in the form of a cough from upstairs, a creaking floorboard, a squeaky drawer, a break in a

171

snore pattern. Disorientation is rarer, thinks Tyrone, but not unheard of. Not when, by definition, you're stumbling around in the dark in a stranger's house.

This is a slightly unusual set up, though, to be fair.

He breathes hard again, gathers himself. Wishes Bags was still here.

At least it's quiet without him. All he can hear is the gentle crumpling of mouldy paper beneath his feet, and the sound of his own breathing.

He holds his breath.

The breathing sounds continue.

Bullshit.

It's just the fear fucking with you.

He forces himself forward, towards the next corner, following the path of floating dust motes in the weak torch beam.

The breathing sound gets louder.

Bullshit.

Still no CDs. No vinyl. Maybe Bags was right, maybe there's nothing but old papers and books here. And it fucking stinks. He's wasting his time. He should just get the fuck out.

He'll just check round this corner. This last corner. Check round there.

If there's nothing, then he's leaving. Straight back out. The way he came in.

The breathing is getting louder.

Bullshit.

Just check the corner man. You can just glance round, innit. Check and then go.

Tyrone pushes his head and the torch around the corner.

The breathing sound is loud, like its right ahead of him, just there.

The torch picks out more dust motes, walls of paper up to the ceiling.

Tyrone sighs. Relief.

But the breathing sound is just there. At his feet.

He drops the torch beam on to the floor. At his feet.

A figure sits there, surrounded by papers and unwashed mugs, plates. It is sitting, apparently cross-legged, just inches from his feet. Its face is hidden as its head is tilted forward, a mess of greasy lank hair and pale white skin.

Its shoulders rise and fall, slowly, in time with the breathing sound.

Tyrone takes a step back, stands on a particularly loud piece of paper.

The head jerks back, a flash of eyes.

Tyrone screams, falls backwards into wall of magazines and comics, now knowing for certain that it's every bit as fragile and unsupportive as it looks – although far heavier – as it collapses on top of him.

The last thing he sees, flashed in the tumbling torchlight before he blacks out, is the cartoon face of some fascist cop, his eyes hidden by a helmet, a speech bubble screaming in bold text 'YOUR MOVE, CREEP!

"Sangita?" Beryle peers around at her from behind a tower of paper. "There's a gentleman here to see you, from the, um, Ministry of Culture."

"'The Ministry of Culture'? There's a Ministry of Culture?"

"There certainly is, Mrs Chandak." Another head appears from behind the tower: late 40s, bald, smart dark suit, slightly forced smile. He extends a hand. "William Jackson-Marsh. Call me Will, please."

"Nice to meet you, Will. Sangita, please." She rises, takes his hand. Shunts the pile of paperwork to one side so she can get a good look at him. He's far better turned out then anybody these days has any real right to be. Sangita feels, for the first time she can remember in years, slightly embarrassed by her self-repaired, scruffy, charity shop attire.

"Please, take a seat. I'd offer you some tea, but..." She gestures at a mug of tepid, green, nettle smelling liquid on the desk next to her. "... to be honest, it tastes like piss."

The man laughs, perhaps slightly embarrassed at her frank language. "Yes, I'm... ah, familiar with the local brew. I had a cup on the train down here. Interesting."

"The train? They're running again today?"

"Yes, yes they are. The service is slow and infrequent, but not too unpleasant. Unlike the tea." That slightly forced smile again. He nods at the small tower of paper. "I see we're keeping you busy?"

"Ha, yes. The joys of a paper-filled office, right? I have to say, on the rare occasions we get a visit from Central down here, we're all rather hoping it will be someone telling us we can have some computers again."

"Ah, I'm afraid not. Not my area at all – quite the opposite in fact. But I hear the boys in the Sutton labs are making some progress. But of course we mustn't rush these things. Far too much at stake."

"Of course." Sangita forces a smile herself. She's far from being a conspiracy theorist, but it's pretty clear the Emergency Coalition is either quite happily dragging its feet or, even worse, lying about how bad things really are. "So, the Ministry of Culture? What brings you down to lowly Bristol?"

"One of your cases, in fact. Mr Richard Lewis, 27 Alice Street, Lawrence Hill?" He's reading from a moleskin notebook he's produced from a jacket pocket.

Sangita pauses, surprised. "Yes. Mr Lewis, he's one of mine. Sorry, Will… I'm a little confused?"

"Sorry, my bad." Will flicks some lint from the knee of his immaculately trousered, crossed leg. "You're not familiar with the Ministry and what we do. In fact, the truth is both you and I do surprisingly similar work, in many ways. You're involved in the regathering of our citizens' personal information, and I'm involved in regathering their culture. Their art, entertainment. Their books, music, TV shows, films. Magazines. Their news and history. All that stuff that just vanished in the crash."

"Ah," Sangita sees where he's going. "Thus your interest in Mr Lewis. Well, yes, he certainly does have a lot of newspapers."

"And potentially a lot more of interest, if my sources are to be believed."

"Your sources?"

Will double-taps his nose with his finger, smiles again. Sangita genuinely can't tell if it was a good natured joke or a slightly sinister warning to not probe any further. She decides to act as though it's the latter.

"I'm heading up a special unit on physical culture reclamation," he continues. "We're targeting collectors, enthusiasts – people who have large deposits of cultural data in non-digital forms – that we feel would be of interest to the state and the wider public. Your Mr Lewis has been identified as quite possibly the country's leading hoarder."

Sangita smiles. "Rich would like that. Mr Lewis, I mean. Despite appearances he is very well natured. A great sense of humour, especially about his condition."

"It sounds like you know him well."

"Well, yes. I mean I've been working with him for over three years now. I wish I could spend more time on him, but like everything… I'm spread very thinly. My aim is to get him to part with as much of the paper matter in his house at possible. It's a considerable fire risk, as you can imagine. But it's a long and slow process, getting him to agree to it. I'm no psychologist, and we can't just barge in there and seize it."

"Ah," Will says, looking up from his notebook to match her gaze. "That's perhaps precisely where I can help you."

"I'm sorry?"

"Under the Martial Law act, and as part of the Central Emergency Coalition, the Ministry of Culture has certain powers when it comes to seizing cultural artefacts we deem may be of value to the public. My suspicion is that there's a lot of data in that little house that we should be processing and archiving."

Sangita feels a chill, trembles slightly. "But… but we are talking about Mr Lewis' private, personal property, surely?"

"Of course." He closes his notebook with a gentle clap, but still enough to make Sangita jump. "Although, after the crash, with so many records being lost, so much financial data gone, the definitions of ownership have become a little… elastic, should we say? It's been a bit of a free for all in a lot of areas, survival of the fittest. Starting from scratch, not so much 'the crash' as 'the reboot', as some of my colleagues say."

He spots the look of unease on Sangita's face, and changes tack slightly.

"Plus, of course, as you've said yourself, it's a considerable fire risk. That paper needs to come out of there, and we might as well have a good look at it before it gets needlessly pulped. Really Sangita, look at it this way – I, and the Ministry, are here to help you. And I'm sure in return you'll be happy to help us back." That forced smile again.

"Of course," she replies, forcing her own. "I'm always happy to help."

Tyrone awakes into a world of stink and paper.

Blinks.

He's looking down into his lap, like he'd passed out with his back against something, his legs covered in lurid sci-fi comics; fascist cops, blue-skinned soldiers, mutant bounty hunters.

He picks one up, stares at it until its bold black lines and words come into focus, lets it drop from his hand on to the others.

His head hurts, his mouth tastes slightly of blood. He explores with his tongue, a cut lip. Nothing major, he's had far worse.

Around him the paper still towers, including most of the one he fell into. It looks different in this light – what light? Is it daylight? He's not sure, but that sounds doubtful – there's no windows to be seen, and whoever lives here never seems to have their curtains open. So there must be electricity today. He should be at home, making use of it, working his machines.

He should get home before the cops come.

But he's so fucking tired. I'll go inna bit.

His head feels heavy, leaning forward...

I'll go

Eyelids feel heavier though...

Inna

Bit

"Are you awake? Do you need a doctor?"

The voice seems a bit on edge, but friendly enough. It's not Bags. Or his mum.

"You've had a bump to the head, I think. Are you okay?"

Blinks.

Tyrone looks up into a pale face, lank, long greasy hair, stained clothes. Eyes just that side of being wild.

A hand extends down to him, touches his upper arm.

"GET THE FUCK OFF ME, MAN! DON'T YOU FUCKING TOUCH ME, YEAH?"

"All right! All right! Sorry!"

Tyrone tries to crawl backwards, like a dog wiping its arse on the carpet, but what's left of the tower of comics he fell into blocks his way. He looks round, no easy escape route. He's going to have to go through this guy that's standing above him. Which shouldn't be too hard, because he's skinny as all fuck.

Although he's got that edge to him, that mad edge. Mad people worry Tyrone. Unpredictable.

Which is even more reason to get going.

He tries to summon energy, can't find it. His head is still heavy.

"Do you want me to get you a doctor?"

"Are the cops coming?"

The guy looks startled, even more so than when Tyrone just shouted at him. He jumps back.

"The cops? Where? Coming here?"

"Did you call them?" Tyrone touches the back of his head, there's a bump. "Did you call the cops? Did you go outside and ring the bell?"

"No. God no. I didn't ring the bell. Then the cops would have come." The guy seems to calm down again, almost instantly. "I fucking hate the cops."

"You do?"

"Yeah. Fucking bastards. The lot of 'em. Come round here and just give me shit they do. I hate the cops."

"Aight. Then me and you are probably going to get on aight then." Tyrone relaxes a little. No cops.

178

"Are you okay? I could go and ring the bell –"

"No! No bell man."

"– and a doctor might come."

"Nah, nah I'm fine. Don't need a doctor. I just need to get up."

"Oh, yeah, right." The guy extends his hand again, and this time Tyrone takes it, lets him help him up to his feet. He sways slightly, a combination of weak legs, heavy head and that smell hitting him. He knows where it's from now. He flinches, screwfaces, steps back.

"What's wrong? Do I smell?"

"A little, yeah." Tyrone wipes his hand on his jeans.

"Sorry. Not had a shower for… ages. Months maybe."

"Is it not working? Your shower? A lot of people's ain't. At least not all the time. At least not hot water."

"To be honest I dunno if it's working, it's full of newspapers." The guy laughs.

"Yeah, well you certainly got a lot of newspapers."

"Yeah, I have, ain't I?" The guy looks around the room, almost like he's seeing it all for the first time, a sincere look of utter disbelief. He looks back at Tyrone and shrugs. "What's that all about?"

Tyrone shrugs back, and laughs. The guy laughs too. They both laugh, shaking their heads.

When they stop, Tryone looks at the guy. He might be a bit mad, but he's aight.

"You're aight man" he says.

"Thanks! My name is Rich."

"Hey, Rich," Tyrone hesitates, not sure if he should reciprocate. Fuck it. "I'm Tyrone."

"Hey, Tyrone. You from round here?"

"Yeah, Barton Hill."

"Up in the towers?"

"Yeah. Up in the towers." Suddenly the small talk seems awkward. "So, Rich, yeah, I should probably get back there, man."

"Oh really? That's a shame." Rich looks genuinely disappointed. "I was going to offer you a cuppa."

"You got tea?"

"Yeah. Well... no. Just that usual stuff."

"The nettles shit?"

"Yeah. The nettles shit."

"Ah, I'm all right, man. Thanks for the offer, though." Tyrone is looking around the room again, at the towers of paper, trying to work out if there's an easy way out.

"Oh, that's all right. Anytime. Come back anytime. It's a shame you gotta leave..."

"Yeah, sorry man, but y'know how it is... things to do..." He's not really got anything to do. He starts to feel a bit guilty. "And, y'know, sorry about breaking in and that."

"Yeah... I was going to ask you about that actually." Rich squints at him. "Breaking in here, it seems like a bit of a weird thing to do?"

"It – that – it... it seems like a weird thing to do? What, weirder than filling your home up with all these fucking newspapers?"

They both laugh again. Tyrone can't quite get his head round it all – maybe he's got concussion – but he's starting to like this Rich guy.

"So why then? Why the newspapers?"

Rich sighs, shakes his head. "I dunno really. At first... it seemed really important. Like all these papers and magazines were being printed and just thrown away. It didn't seem right.

Like what happens to the information in them when they're gone?"

"This was before the crash?"

"Yeah. Before the crash – I mean, before the crash I was going to scan them all, then I could have thrown them away. But then the crash happened... and it seemed even more important. All that information gone, I couldn't let this all go too." Rich shakes his head again. "That probably sounds crazy."

"Nah, it doesn't." Tyrone says, sincerely. "It makes a lot of sense actually."

"Do you remember the crash? Were you too young?"

"Yeah... I remember it." Tyrone feels that strange loss he gets, that feeling of missing out on something, that nostalgia for something he never really had in the first place. "Yeah, I remember it. Vaguely. I was about six. I remember all my toys stopped working, my spex. The TV." He laughs, but sadly.

"You never answered my question!" Rich says, as if sensing Tyrone's mood and trying to cheer him up.

"Your question?"

"Yeah! Why'd you break in here then? Did you want some newspapers?"

Tyrone laughs. "Nah man, not papers. I was looking for vinyls."

"Vinyls?"

"Yeah. Vinyls. Tapes even. CDs."

"Oh records? Music? That's all through here."

Tyrone is confused. Rich seems to be pointing at yet another wall of boxes and newspapers, yet another unlikely cliff chiselled out of consumer pre-history.

And then he's climbing up the face of it, and Tyrone realises he's heading for a narrow gap up near the ceiling, about a metre wide but barely a foot high – the top of a doorway, the rest of it bricked up by what looks like split shoeboxes full of crushed 3D-printed junk. Toys, trinkets, souvenirs from a failed state. Forgotten hardcopies of stuff that doesn't exist any more. Rich is up it incredibly quickly, finding impossible footholds. Before he knows it, Tyrone is watching the worn soles of his trainers as they disappear through the tiny gap, followed by the sound of something falling to the floor.

A beat. "You coming through?"

Tyrone forces back the urge to run again, to flee to some normality, and just shrugs instead. "Yeah, aight. Hang on." He's got through smaller windows, he figures, and usually for far less interesting prospects. This mad old geezer might actually have some beats back there.

A few minutes of scrambling and climbing later, and Tyrone drops into another tiny, claustrophobic space that he guesses must have once been the house's kitchen. Rich is standing above him, arms outstretched, a slightly manic grin across his pale face.

"Look! Music!"

Tyrone looks around him, trembling slightly, trying to take it all in.

The room, like the rest of the house, is stacked to the ceiling, but as Tyrone focuses on the walls he feels the hairs on the back of his neck start to prick up. This isn't another deposit of random magazines and papers; most of the walls are built up from stacked vinyl records, piled on top of each other, or precarious towers of CDs in plastic jewel cases.

"You shouldn't store your vinyls like this," he hears himself saying, a near-forgotten echo of his lost mother's words. "Flat on top of each other. The weight will squash out the grooves."

"I know," sighs Rich. "But I've got no choice, really. I mean I thought I'd make some special storage system and…"

Tyrone isn't listening any more – he's kneeling on the ground, flicking through a selection of albums that are stored correctly – about 40 or so, leaning against a wall of what seems to be infinitely more.

His hands shake as he works his way through them.

Public Enemy, Coldplay, The Clash, Dire Straits, Miles Davis, Nine Inch Nails, The Beatles, Tackhead, Debussy...

... Some are names he recognises, some he doesn't...

... Bob Marley and The Wailers, 50 Cent, Portishead, Run DMC, Soul II Soul...

"You got any idea how much these are all worth now?" he asks. "There... there must be a fortune here."

"Yeah, I guess. But... they're mine. All of them. I don't want to sell them." There's palpable anxiety in his voice.

Tyrone is still flicking.

Until he hits something, something he recognises, an image burned into his memory.

He'd seen it so many times, floating in the air in their lounge, a 12-inch wide translucent square of scanned cover art spinning slowly as his mother's spex wirelessly pumped the beats, the atmospherics, the vocals and the melancholy around their tiny little flat.

And from the kitchen, her voice, singing along as she prepared dinner.

She was still singing those songs years later, even after the crash came and stole her music.

She was still singing them up until the end, when the winter came and stole her life.

That darkened bedroom, echoing with coughs, curtains drawn. When his aunt took him in there, led him by the hand, she would struggle to stay awake for a short time, just so she could smile at him. Just so she could sing to him, in that croaky whisper.

Tyrone feels hot tears on his cheeks, tries to wipe them away without Rich seeing him, fights the urge to run again. There's nowhere to run to anyway, not from this.

He looks up, his mouth dry. "Can we listen to these?"

"Of course!" Rich steps to one side, reveals a turntable and CD player on the floor – ancient, pre-digital, too old to be infected. Alongside them is a battered amp and speakers. "What do you want to listen to?"

Tyrone pulls the record out from the stack, hands the all too familiar sleeve to Rich, feeling the weight of the vinyl inside. He can smell it. He takes one last glance at its brown cover, the red diamond across its face, the strange fire emblem and the huge, lower case letters – 'massive attack'.

"Can we listen to this?"

"So this is it? This is the place?"

"Yes, this is it," Sangita climbs down from the cab of the council van, her legs weak. It's been a while since she travelled in a motor vehicle; even in her position it's rare. She smiles at the local kids who are crowding around it, who had been following them on foot since they turned off St Philips Causeway. It's an even rarer sight for them.

Will is at the terrace house's worn front door by now, like an excited kid at pre-crash Christmas. The obnoxious prick. She sighs and catches up to him.

He's knocking on the door, no answer. Impatiently he knocks again.

"It can take Mr Lewis a while to answer the door. You'll understand when you see how it is in there."

Will knocks again anyway.

"What's that noise? Can you hear that?"

Sangita strains to listen. Something is vibrating the house, shaking glass and brick, a deep bass tone.

"It sounds like music," she says.

"Then if he's listening to music, he won't be able to hear us knocking." Will tries the door handle. It's unlocked.

"I don't think we should —"

Too late; Will has pushed open the door. He's in. Sangita sighs to herself and follows.

He hasn't got far. He's standing in the hallway, transfixed, staring at the walls of stacked papers and boxes that seem to remodel the very architecture of the tiny house. He runs a hand down one stack, eyes wide, voice hushed in awe. "Incredible."

She pushes past him, beyond tired of his bullshit. Inside the music is clearer, louder — that bassline still rolling through everything, a woman's voice soaring above it. She has to shout.

"Rich? Are you home? It's Sangita. I have someone here to see you."

There's a muffled call back, followed by the sound of clambering, some mild cursing, and then Rich appears from around a corner, a beaming smile across his face.

"Oh, hi Sangita. Sorry I didn't hear you come in, we were in the music room."

"Music room? You've got music here?" Will's little face is all lit up.

"Oh yeah, loads of music. Come and see!"

Sangita is more interested in something else he said. "*We?*"

As if on cue someone else emerges from around the corner, some black kid in a scruffy hoody, looking nervous. Shifty. A long scar runs down his left cheek, ruining his otherwise perfect teenage complexion. Sangita knows what that means. Trouble.

"Who are you? What's going on here?" she asks him.

185

"This is Tyrone," says Rich. "He's my friend. We've been listening to music."

Tyrone stays silent, looks even more nervous. Sangita can't be sure, but he looks like he might have been crying.

Will extends a hand out to Rich, who shakes it warmly, while he introduces himself. "It's an impressive collection you've got here."

"Thank you! Is that why you're here, to have a look at it?"

Will goes to reply, but Sangita jumps in first. Time to try and take control.

"Now, Richard, Mr Jackson-Marsh here is from the Ministry of Culture up in London. He's come all the way down here to help you move your stuff out of the house, so it's safer. So there's no fires."

"Move it where?"

"Up to London, Mr Lewis," says Will. "Where it'll all be processed and then stored in a proper archive. And then –"

"No!" says Rich.

"Well –"

"No. I'm not happy about that, no. Sorry. This is my private property. It's going nowhere. Especially not fucking London. Horrible place."

"Okay, Rich," injects Sangita, "Let's not get ahead of –"

"No. Sorry. It's not going anywhere. This is my private property."

"Yeah, man," Tyrone speaks up, "this is all his stuff. You can't just come in here and steal it. What the fuck?"

"Please, keep out of this," says Sangita.

"It's not stealing." Will produces a piece of folded paper from the inside of his jacket. It's the first Sangita has seen of it. "This is a warrant issued by the Ministry of Culture, signed by the chief secretary of the Emergency Coalition. It gives me the power to seize the contents of this house as an asset for the Public Reconstruction Archives. It gives you twenty-four hours from my issuing it to you to get your personal belongings in order –"

"These ARE my personal belongings."

"– It gives you twenty-four hours to remove a reasonable amount of your personal belongings from the house before we return and take everything we see fit to."

"No."

"I'm afraid there is no 'no', Mr Lewis."

"Rich, please. Don't fight this. I'm not too happy about this either, but you know it has to happen. You know you can't keep all this… stuff here." Sangita gestures at the stacked contents of the hall. "It's not safe, Rich. We've been talking about it for years. What if there's a fire? You know how long it takes for a fire crew to get here, it's not like before –"

"No." Rich is adamant, firm. "No. Sorry. Not like this, and not to London. Now, please, I'd like you both to leave."

"You heard him," says Tyrone, pushing past Rich in the narrow hallway. "He asked you to leave. So leave."

Will sneers. "I've no idea who you think –"

"He said LEAVE," Tyrone pushes him in the chest, with what looks like relatively little effort, but apparently enough force to send him out of the open front door. He follows him out, pushes him again. This time it's enough to send him sprawling on to pavement. The small crowd that had gathered around the van quickly reassembles itself around the prone civil servant.

Will sits up, shaken. "You've just made a grave mistake."

"Yeah? You think? No surprises here, it's what I do best. And I'm just about to do it again." Tyrone raises his right foot off the ground, swings it back, aimed at Will's head – Before he can move, his way is blocked by a slab of wood, forced straight across his chest.

"No more mistakes today Tyrone, that's enough."

Tyrone knows this voice all too well. Street Magistrate Kohli: seven feet of intimidation topped off with a dark navy turban, his plastic-sealed badge pinned to the chest of his black, full-length overcoat. His arm extends out, holding Tyrone back with one of his signature twin cricket bats. At his shoulder is Special Constable Dajani, her eyes piercing out from under her hijab, one hand clutching the grip of her still-sheathed but famed katana.

Tyrone steps back. You don't fuck with the judges.

"You know this child, Magistrate Kohli?" asks Sangita.

"Yeah, I know him. He's Tyrone Cooper. He's a thief."

"Then arrest him." Will pulls himself to his feet, visibly shaken, dusting off his suit.

"What for?"

"Assault! He assaulted me!"

"And you are?"

"William Jackson-Marsh. From the Ministry of Culture."

Kohli's eyes narrow. "There's a Ministry of Culture?"

"So he says. Says he's gonna take all Rich's stuff." Tyrone points at Will from behind the cricket bat barrier. "Who's a fucking thief now?"

Kohli still has his eyes on Will. He knows Tyrone, but if there's anybody he trusts less than Lawrence Hill looters it's suited men from London. "Is this true? You're taking this man's belongings?"

Will hands him the piece of paper. "Here. Read for yourself, Magistrate. It's all outlined there. Yes, I'll be back tomorrow to take this man's property. As of then, it'll no longer belong to him, but to the state." He brushes dust of his otherwise still immaculate suit. "Everybody needs to remember: we're all in this together."

And with that he turns and heads back to the van, Sangita in tow, apologetically smiling at Kohli as she goes.

The crowd watches the ancient van splutter into life and move off. This time the kids don't run after it.

There's a stunned silence for a few seconds, and then Tyrone breaks it.

"You can't let them do this man! You're meant to protect us!"

"Quiet, Tyrone." Kohli is reading.

"Look!" Tyrone is pointing at Rich, who is sitting on his doorstep, head in his hands, rocking back at forward, distressed. "Look at him! He ain't done nothing to anyone, and these fuckers just turn up and say they're gonna take all his shit?"

"Quiet, Tyrone."

"Quiet? You really gonna let them just do this? How... how many looters have you taken out with those bats, man? How many thieves has she marked with that sword of hers?" Tyrone's hand reflexively goes to the scar on his cheek, until he pulls it away, disgusted. "And you're gonna just stand there, and let him walk all over you –"

"Quiet, Tyrone! For fuck's sake... I'm trying to read this." Kohli sighs, stroking his beard. "There... might be something we can do. According to this. I don't know... maybe. But we'll have to work quick. Dajani – go and ring the bell. I want everybody out here. Then we'll decide what to do."

"Look, its fucked, fam." Bags holds the mess of broken metal spokes and pink plastic that was once a kid's umbrella up to Rich's face. "Look. It's fucking broken. It's going in the bin."

Rich is clearly agitated. "You never know when it might come in handy –"

"Handy? *Handy?* What's handy about this? What you gonna do with this if it rains? Get wet, that's what, bruv."

189

"You could use it for spare parts, they don't make them any more."

"Bruv, they don't make ANYTHING any more."

"It's all right Bags, back off man." Tyrone appears, moving in between the two. "Look, Rich, I know this is hard for you man, yeah? But we gotta move FAST. They're gonna be back here in a few hours. And we ain't got time to take everything. So either some stuff goes in the bin, or you leave it here and those government fuckers take it. Now which would you rather?"

Rich looks at the floor, shaking his head. "The bin."

Tyrone smiles, grasps Rich by his upper arm. "Good man. It's gonna be all right bruv, aight?"

"Aight," says Rich, smiling for the first time that morning.

Tyrone laughs. "Why don't you go make another round of tea, yeah?"

Rich smiles again, heads to the – now far more accessible – kitchen.

"Is it really gonna be all right?" asks Bags.

"Fuck knows, man. Kohli reckons so." He looks around the room, which has been largely emptied now. A woman he knows just by sight, who lives in one of the towers, is clearing up a few loose sheets of paper in the corner. It's weird to be able to see carpet. "I hope so. Everyone's come out and helped, y'know? Everyone's gonna be gutted if it don't work."

"Gutted? People are gonna be more than gutted. There's gonna be a fucking riot."

Tyrone doesn't answer Bags, just nods and watches him walk out, carrying another box of junk, the broken pink umbrella balanced on top. At the doorway he steps aside to let the huge mass of Magistrate Kohli come in.

"How's it looking?" he asks Tyrone.

"Yeah, all right. We getting there. Well, down here at least. Truth is I ain't even looked upstairs yet." He glances up at the ceiling.

"How's Mr Lewis taking it?"

"Rich?" Tyrone shrugs. "He's all right. He's coping. Every so often he has a little freak out at someone and I have to calm him down. I mean he knows this needs doing, but he's lived like this for too long, y'know? He knows it ain't quite right but... I dunno. Having to change in just one day. It's hard for him, man."

"You're doing a good thing, Tyrone, helping him. It's a good thing for him and the whole community."

"I hope so." Tyrone knows he's right, but can't shake the feeling he's not being completely selfless in this. He wants to get his hands on those vinyls again.

Kohli turns to leave, but stops – looks back at Tyrone from over his shoulder.

"You know I knew your mum, right?"

Tyrone does. Kohli has brought it up before, in the past. Never for good reasons. He nods at him, silently.

"Yeah, well if she could see you now, doing this – she'd be proud of you, Tyrone."

"I've always had my reservations about the Street Magistrates program," Will says, climbing out of the cab of the van.

"Really?" Sangita just wants this all to end now, so that this suit-shaped sack of shit will fuck off back to London. "We all had our reservations at the time, but Central always insisted it was the only way of keeping order. Certainly sending the army into Bristol didn't quite work out as planned."

"Yeah, but it just creates trumped up little Hitlers. Like this Kohli, for example. A little power has gone to his head. He probably wants to introduce sharia law."

Sangita squints at him. "I doubt it. He's a sikh."

"Whatever, he's out of his fucking depth now."

Will is striding confidently towards Rich's house, the three council workers carrying packaging crates following closely behind him. Sangita pauses in the street, looks up and down the row of terraced houses. It's quiet. Very quiet. In fact, there's nobody around at all. Sangita shrugs. So much for there being trouble. Good. They can get this done quick, Will can go back to London, and she can go back to the office, back to pushing pieces of paper around and drinking piss flavoured nettle tea.

One of the council guys is knocking on Rich's front door, but before there's a chance for anyone to answer Will has pushed it open. They all follow him in.

Into the hallway. The empty hallway.

They all stand there in silence, confused.

"Hello?" A voice. They all follow where it seems to come from.

Into the front room. The empty front room.

It's not completely empty. Far across what now feels like a vast plain of previously unseen distressed carpet, sitting in a lone armchair, is Rich. He's reading a newspaper.

"Hello!" he says, raising a mug up for them all to see. "Who wants a cuppa?"

Silence.

"Well," Sangita says finally, glancing around the empty space, "Good work Rich. This is... very good. Very clean. And safe. Very safe. No fire risks here. Very good."

"Thanks!"

"What have you done?" says Will.

"Sorry?"

"I said what have you done, you fucking retard? Where is everything?"

"Everything?"

Sangita finds herself backing away from Will, fearing his head might explode.

"Yes, EVERYTHING. All the fucking... stuff... all the books, the toys. The music. All the fucking newspapers."

Rich smiles and holds up the newspaper he's been reading. "You can have this one if you want. I've nearly finished it."

"The rest of them, you fucking idiot. Where's the rest of them?"

"Oh, we moved them."

"Where? Where did you move them too?"

"Down the street" Rich says cheerfully. "Into the community centre."

Will stares at him for a second, then turns and storms out – Sangita and the confused council workers following him. A few minutes later, he's pushing his way through the heavy double doors into Lawrence Hill Community Centre – too quickly to notice, unlike Sangita, that someone has altered the sign at the front of the building. The word 'Centre' has been crossed through with paint, and the word 'Library' added next to it.

All five of them freeze as they enter.

There's electricity today, and the interior of the building is brightly lit. Music fills the room from stereo speakers at the back of the room – Sangita thinks she recognises it; Miles Davis. It makes her smile.

The rest of the room is full of people and tables, upon which Rich's newspapers and magazines are clearly stacked. Some of the people seem to be sorting through them, separating them from matted messes and organising them into new piles. Others seem to just be reading them, or chatting quietly amongst themselves. On the floor some kids are playing with broken plastic toys, their faces full of preoccupied glee.

"What the hell is this?" says Will.

From behind one of the nearest tables Magistrate Kohli rises, closing the faded newspaper he's been reading. He looks straight past Will as he speaks.

"Mrs Chandak – the community has got together and helped Mr Lewis clear out his house. I hope it'll be to your liking now, it should no longer pose a fire risk."

Sangita smiles and nods. "Yes, thank you, Magistrate. I just saw it, it's more than satisfactory. Thank you, and everyone. Good work." She notices the scarred boy, Tyrone, standing behind Kohli, and smiles at him too.

"Yes, very good." The frustration in Will's voice is palpable. "Thank you. But we'll take over from here." He gestures to one of the crate-carrying council workers.

"I'm afraid not," says Kohli. "All of this will be staying here."

"Nonsense. You've seen the warrant, Magistrate. This is now all the property of the Ministry of Culture."

"I have seen your piece of paper, Mr Jackson-Marsh. And I have one to give you. Tyrone?"

Tyrone walks over to the suited man, hands him a piece of paper. It's been badly typed on a manual writer, with three scrawled signatures at the bottom.

"What's this?"

"That is an ownership transfer form. Under the Emergency Martial Law Act, it allows an individual to legally transfer an item or items of property to another individual or organisation." Kohli talks slowly, clearly enjoying the theatrics.

Will drops it to the floor. "This is worthless." Tyrone bites his tongue.

"Actually, it's not. It's a very useful form for us Magistrates, very helpful when resolving property disputes. And Coalition issued."

"Whatever. You're wasting my time. I'm seizing – as per that warrant – all of this stuff."

"Again, I'm afraid not. It seems I may be more familiar with your warrant than you are." Kohli produces his copy of the piece of paper from inside his overcoat. "There's a condition here, in the small print – 'This warrant allows Ministry staff to remove what they deem as culturally or historically valuable material from individuals. It does not allow the removal of said materials from organisations, institutions or facilities which provide free access to them to the local community or wider public.' Mr Lewis signed ownership over to the Lawrence Hill community. Welcome to the newly opened Lawrence Hill Community Library."

Will is stunned for a moment, silent. Then he laughs, sneers. "Bullshit." He turns to the council worker nearest him. "Start packing all this stuff up."

The guy looks at him, glances round the room, "I dunno, man..."

"Fuck's sake!" Will snatches the crate from him, and steps forward.

From out of the shadows behind him there's a shnniccckt sound, a glint of steel. Will freezes as the end of the samurai sword touches his nose, stops his movement. He holds his breath as its tip playfully caresses his cheek.

"I wouldn't take another step," Dijani says calmly, the sly hint of a grin on her face, "unless you want me to mark you, thief."

It's getting dark as Tyrone, hood up, walks briskly back across the allotments to the light-studded towers. There's electricity today, and he should be working his ancient machines, making new beats.

Someone calls his name behind him and he spins round. It's Rich, out of breath from trying to catch up with him, carrying a shopping bag.

"Have they gone?"

"Yeah, man, they've gone. Kohli and Dijani saw them off. It was pretty cool."

"Do you think they'll come back?"

"Maybe. Who knows. I hope not. We'll be ready if they do."

"Cool. That's cool." Rich stares down at the ground, as he does when he's nervous.

Tyrone looks at the old guy, feels a sudden wave of guilt. "Rich, you're happy with all this, right?"

"With what?"

"With signing all your stuff over to the community?"

"Oh. Sure. Yeah. I mean... I was a bit not sure at first, but now I'm sure. It's better. There's more space there, and everyone gets to use the information. That's what it's all about really, what I wanted, I think. There's just one thing..."

"What, man?"

Rich shuffles nervously again. "Now it's all sorted, Tyrone... will you still come and visit me?"

Tyrone laughs. "Of course, man, of course I will."

Rich smiles. "Good. Oh, I wanted to give you this, to say thank you." He hands Tyrone the plastic shopping bag.

"You don't need to give me anything, man."

"No, I do. I want to. Please."

Tyrone takes the bag.

"I want you to have it, because I know you like that one."

Tyrone reaches inside, pulls the record out from of the bag, stares at the all too familiar sleeve, feeling the weight of the vinyl inside. He can smell it. He looks at Rich and then back at its brown cover, the red diamond across its face, the strange fire emblem and the huge, lower case letters – 'massive attack'.

He wants to hug him, but all he manages is to whisper thank you, and then he turns and walks away, a warm tear running down the scar on his cheek.

EPILOGUE

[citation needed]
Ken MacLeod

The risers of the twenty-five or so outside steps up from the esplanade to The Lie Dispensary are painted like the spines of books. Most are dystopias or other socially conscious classics: *The Women's Room, The Grapes of Wrath, The Female Man, Trainspotting…* The paint's a hard waterproof gloss, and just as well: a spring tide can swamp the Huxley and the Orwell, and storm surges splash the Atwood and shingle the Bradbury.

There's a boxy porch at the top, through which a right-angle turn to a small hallway offers the choice of an indoor stair to the roof-top restaurant, or an entrance to the right. That takes you to the café bar, from which you can go to the bookstore (straight ahead, past the bar counter) and the library (off to the left, just by the bar counter).

We usually treat guest writers to a pre-event dinner and drinks in the roof restaurant. That evening, I and my husband Mark were entertaining – or rather, being entertained by – Fred Chang. He's older than he looks in the author photos (all writers are, being generally vain and lazy) but his wrinkles emphasise the vivacity of his expressions. Getting him for a reading and signing was for us a big deal, even though two of the chain bookstores wouldn't deign to have him. "I'm world famous," he once said, "in a very small world."

In case that small world doesn't include you... Chang writes two kinds of science fiction. The first, that makes him money, is space opera. The second, that makes him famous, is offbeat speculative short stories: quirky fables which have been compared (never by him) to the space fictions of Stanislaw Lem and the 'Cosmicomics' of Italo Calvino. My own view, for what it's worth, is that he does emulate these masters in literary form but not, perhaps, in literary quality.

While we ate chips and sipped cola, Chang nibbled dim sum, glugged Tsingtao, and held forth, amusingly as ever. All the while I kept half an eye on the camera feeds in the bottom left of my specs.

Everything was going well, place filling up, yet another customer climbing the steps...

"Uh oh," I said.

"What?" said Mark.

The man was young, lean and fit. He wore one of those leather caps with fur and flaps. Beard, fluorescent jacket, Lycra top, jeans, flashy trainers: cycle-courier type. But he ascended like an old person, step by wary step. As my gaze flicked from camera to camera, I could see that he was checking the title on each riser.

"Ministry," I said.

"Sure?"

I twiddled a forefinger, peering at face recognition. "Hang on."

The name came up tardily through buffering: Victor Hutchison. Science degree. Self-employed. Age 22. But long experience – my own and my apps' – flagged that his online footprint was thin and inconsistent. The Ministry is stretched and it skimps, especially on one-shot missions: eager volunteers, in it for the credit and a small cash payment. This probably meant Hutchison was here to show their hand, not just report back.

"Excuse me," I said, shoving my plate of chips towards Mark. I nodded to Chang – who returned my glance with a wry seen-it-all look – and picked up my cola bottle. "Time for me to mingle."

Hutchison paused in the boxy porch at the top to make a note, and went through to the café bar. I drifted after him. (Long hair, long skirt, both faded – I give good drift.) A dozen tables are small and round, inviting intimacy; two are long, encouraging conversation. Nearly all were occupied. Cutlery clattered, and voices loud or quiet chattered. Smells of coffee and beer and the fruity whiff of vape wafted.

Hutchison swept the room with a glance, perhaps recognising a few faces. We had a respectable sprinkling of writers and critics through the crowd tonight. He didn't clock me coming in, and passed, as far as I could tell, unrecognised. He strolled past the counter to the bookshop. Less busy than the café, it felt almost as crowded – there isn't much room to move about, except sideways. A long table with stackable chairs around it occupies the middle of the room, and for that evening yet more chairs were huddled in rows at the far end. Near the till, two young women were piling books in two columns that towered like stereo speakers at the head of the table.

Favouring the young ladies with a vague smile, Hutchison sidled past them and began a systematic survey of the stock. The books are arranged alphabetically by author. Aarons, Aaronson… Left to right, top to bottom, Hutchison worked his way crabwise from case to case and wall to wall. I chatted to our two assistants, my back to our unwelcome visitor, and watched. We have a tiny camera at the back of each shelf, its lens unnoticeable as a pin-head, and more in the ceiling. Now and then his hand darted out, snaring a suspect title – *True History of the Kelly Gang, Swimming with Seals, Lanark, One Day in the Life of Ivan Denisovich, The Moment of Eclipse, Middlesex* – to flick through the pages and put them back.

Hutchison stood up from a study of the final bottom shelf (Zelazny, Zamyatin) and ducked into the library. After a discreet moment, I followed him. Like the café, the library has tables where people eat and drink (and, at less busy times of the day, read). Like the shop, its walls are lined with shelves. The books are old, and arranged... well, I know where to find any of them.

Hutchison stood before a shelf of blue-spined paperbacks: Pelican Classics. *The Law of Freedom*, *The Wealth of Nations*, *A Vindication of the Rights of Women*, *Man versus the State*, *The Rights of Man*, *Leviathan*, *The Fable of the Bees*... He must have recognised them all from his digital check-list. I wandered among the tables, nodding and chatting to diners. He pounced on *Reflections on the Revolution in France*, turned over the first few yellowed leaves, and replaced the book.

Perhaps he was reassured by its publication date. Where does the Ministry find these people?

By the time my random walk intersected his progress around the walls, Hutchison was gazing at old linguistics textbooks. As if inadvertently, I stood beside him in a narrow gap between shelves and chair-backs, getting in his way.

"Looking for anything in particular?" I asked.

He turned from baffled scrutiny of Chomsky's *Lectures on Government and Binding*. For a moment I could measure his exact lack of interest in an old lady peering at him through round glasses. Then something clicked, whether in his recall of his briefing or (educated guess) in a drop-down menu in the folded-down peak of his cap, and his eyes widened.

"Ah!" he said. "You must be Mrs –"

"Matilde," I said firmly. "So... What are you looking for, Victor?"

A flicker of bewilderment: this was probably the first time he'd been addressed by that name.

"Oh! Nothing. I'm just here for the Fred Chang event."

"Starts in half an hour," I said. "We have his books on sale next door, and you have time to catch a drink."

"I'm puzzled," he said. "You... circulate books like this?"

"Of course not," I said. "I'm a bookseller, yes, but these books aren't for sale. They don't circulate. This room is a library. My library, as it happens."

"Do you lend them out?"

I shrugged. "There's no law against lending books to friends."

He frowned. "Well actually, there is, if it's... you know, terrorist material."

I sucked cola through the paper straw and gave him an innocent look.

"You won't find, say, the Penguins by James Connolly, Carlos Marighella, Che Guevara or Bill 'Yank' Levy on these shelves," I said.

His eyes rolled as he hurriedly looked up names, and widened as he found them.

"Anyway," I added, edging door-ward, "I have to attend to set-up. See you at the event, and in the meantime – enjoy your browsing!"

He almost grabbed my elbow.

"But–but suppose someone nicked any of these books? Would they be lost forever?"

"We have state-of-the-art surveillance," I told him, over my shoulder. "And if someone got past it, or if any of these books were otherwise removed," – I guessed what was on his mind – "all of lasting interest have been online for nearly a century." Another innocent blink. "So I'm told."

Standing room only: about fifty. Mark conducted Fred Chang to his place. He chose not to sit, as I delivered the needs-no-introduction introduction.

Chang opened his hands to the round of applause. "Thank you, Matilde! Thank you, Mark! Thank you, Lie Dispensary!

Thank you all!" He patted each book-stack like the heads of well-behaved children. "My latest novel, *Blood on a Black Comet*, and my back catalogue. I hope you buy and read them, and I'll be delighted to sign afterwards. I see some new faces, and some familiar faces. Some of you, I know, have read – and heard me read from – every one of my books already. So tonight, I'd like to read from a story of mine which I can be certain none of you has read before: my work in progress, *The Regime of Truth*."

More applause. Hutchison, halfway down the length of the table, sat up a little, eyes alert. Chang leaned forward, one hand on the seat-back, tablet in the other, and read:

"About three hundred and seventy-three light-years from Earth," he began, in a conversational tone, "is a small red star within whose painfully narrow habitable zone swiftly orbits a planet known, in one of the local languages, as Thrakis. The Thrakians, as they do not call themselves, are not at all like human beings. They resemble us in many ways – upright, bipedal, binocular, bisexual and so forth – but having evolved and advanced (not quite the same thing, as you must know) on a world whose day is longer than its year, where solar tides inundate and drain all land but the mountains twice a day, where these same tidal forces fuel frequent and unpredictable volcanic eruptions, and industrial global warming is difficult to distinguish from periodic brushes with the gently pulsating photosphere of the star – the Thrakians, I say, are bound to exhibit marked differences from our species in their social psychology.

"One such difference we may find difficult to credit, or even to imagine. That is: Thrakians have an inclination to believe on insufficient evidence. From the most fleeting rumour to the most elaborate structure of speculation – no matter how absurd, no matter how brief the moment or trivial the effort of thought it would take to dismiss a belief, you will find a significant number, sometimes a majority, of Thrakians believing it. Worse, having once acquired a belief, Thrakians display two unfortunate urges:

to spread the belief to as many others as they can, and to resent and resist any criticism of the belief. Bizarre as we may find it, they treat an attack on their ideas as an attack on their very inmost selves.

"These inclinations – whether genetically innate or socially acquired is still a matter of (predictably impassioned and fruitless) debate – can be understood, however baffling such an alien mentality may seem to us, as a result of the hostile and unpredictable environment in which their species stumbled into self-awareness. Superstitious behaviour, fanatically held belief, and childhood obedience to adult rules no matter how arbitrary, had survival value for the individuals and groups concerned, and for the behaviour patterns themselves.

"Nevertheless, despite their harsh environment and their heavy burden of unfounded and obsolete beliefs, the Thrakians advanced by fits and starts to a high technological civilisation. Their twice-daily isolation on mountain ranges was overcome by – and indeed stimulated – improvements in transport and communication, from the log raft and the smoke signal all the way to the jet hydrofoil and the global computer network. The fundamental tenets of the scientific method of discussion – such as that any idea may be critically examined and belief should be proportioned to the evidence – became firmly established.

"But –!"

Chang paused and raised a forefinger, his gaze sweeping the audience.

"These tenets of rationality," he went on, "were at first only applied in science and industry. Outside these domains – even in the minds of scientists and technologists when their day's work was done – the Thrakians' deep inclination to uncritical belief raged unchecked. Word-spinning philosophers, flea-cracking ideologues, fanatics and demagogues, preachers and prophets, lawyers and politicians – in short, crooks and shysters of all kinds – continued to ply a lucrative trade.

"For many decades and centuries (by our reckoning, of course) the dichotomy was tolerated, even celebrated, and it remained in a sense tolerable. Science and technology continued to advance. However, this very advance made the inclination to uncritical belief ever more dangerous. Global communications enabled false beliefs to spread faster and farther than their refutations. Fanatics and demagogues armed themselves with ever deadlier weapons. Eventually, uncritical belief was turned on and corrupted the scientific method in the service of sinister interests – whose chief weapon was, ironically if predictably, the baseless claim that science itself was an uncritical belief system, corrupted by sinister interests!

"Eventually, after many disasters both natural and social, a new belief arose in one of the richest and mightiest realms of Thrakis. In this realm, political leaders at every level of society were drawn (far more largely than elsewhere) from the ranks of scientists, technologists, industrial managers and engineers. For reasons deep in that realm's turbulent history, the public profession of religious belief by its political leaders was so frowned upon as to be almost unheard of. Furthermore, while public avowal of the prevailing political ideals – or ideology, if you will – was de rigueur, any hint of personal sincerity in that avowal was met among the engineers and their like in the ruling circles with derision at best, suspicion at worst. Sincere belief was anything but a commendation for advancement – quite the opposite in fact!

"As time went on and older generations passed away, the rulers of that realm – and of other realms, eager to emulate what they thought was the secret of its prosperity, and sometimes outstripping their exemplars in zeal – made formal and open declaration of what had hitherto been only implicit. They decreed that henceforth, all public discussion of policy should be based only on peer-reviewed scientific evidence. The decree was rigorously enforced. All religious teachings, all speculations on

Thrakian nature (so different, of course, from human nature) and all deductions from the putative natural rights of Thrakians, and suchlike fancies, were swept from the public square with an iron broom. Their place was taken by empirical social and natural science and the consequences of their results on matters of public weal. All doctrines, ideals, principles, mantras, slogans and commandments were replaced by two simple standards of discussion, dinned into the population from dawn to dusk: 'Evidence and Consequence! Evidence and Consequence!'

"Public worship, philosophical debate, and private belief went largely unmolested. But any appeal to ideas without scientific evidence in matters of public policy, and any discussion in mass and social media of their principles and any implications they might have for policy, were firmly suppressed. This became known as 'the regime of truth', and —"

At this point Hutchinson, who had become increasingly restive, sprang to his feet.

"Stop!" he cried.

There was a murmur of consternation and a clatter of chairs.

"Why?" demanded Chang.

Hutchison was shaking a little, righteousness contending with nervousness. The lad was brave, I'll give him that. It can't be easy to stand up and face the hostility of a roomful of people whose entertainment you've interrupted.

"I'm showing you the red card, Mr Chang!"

And this he literally did, flourishing the red card of the Ministry to make sure everyone saw it. Three people, I'm sorry to say, pushed back their chairs and scurried from the room, faces averted to hide their shame from themselves if no one else.

"Why?" asked Chang again, when the commotion had ceased. "I'm merely reading a work of avowed and obvious fiction – speculative fiction, at that!"

"But it's not fiction," Hutchison said, voice almost cracking. "It's clearly and obviously a satire of the Ministry's public information policy."

Chang raised his eyebrows. "'Clearly and obviously'?"

"Yes, I mean come on, everybody knows…" Hutchison looked around the table, as if for confirmation.

"Prove it," said Chang.

The after-signing drinks and arguments continued long into the evening, until we reluctantly had to call them to a halt because the tide was coming in and had reached the outside steps.

About the Authors

Allen Ashley is an award-winning writer and editor based in London, UK. His most recent book is the poetry collection *Echoes from An Expired Earth* (Demain Publishing, 2020). Allen is the founder of Clockhouse London Writers and is also a former President of the British Fantasy Society.

Contact: allenashley-writer@hotmail.co.uk

Website: www.allenashley.com/

Once in her life, and a long time ago, **Jennifer Marie Brissett** owned and operated a Brooklyn indie bookstore called Indigo Café & Books. Now she is an author and has written the novels *ELYSIUM* (Aqueduct Press) and *Destroyer of Light* (Tor Books, 2020). Her work has been the finalist for a number of awards and has won the Philip K. Dick Special Citation. You can find her short stories in *FIYAH Magazine*, *Fantastic Stories of the Imagination*, *Lightspeed Magazine*, Motherboard Vice, *Uncanny Magazine*, *The Future Fire*, the anthology *APB: Artists against Police Brutality* and other publications. She currently teaches writing and writes and lives in NYC.

Website: www.jennbrissett.com/

Brendan C. Byrne's fiction has appeared in *Terraform*, *DarkMountain*, *Imperica*, *Flapperhouse*, and *FLURB*, his criticism in *Motherboard*, *The Intercept*, *Arc*, *New Scientist*, *The Baffler*, and *Rhizome*. Along with Ingrid Burrington, he received a 2019 Mozilla Creative Media Award for their epistolary newsletter novella *The Training Commission*.

Twitter: @BrendanCByrne

Dan Coxon is an editor and writer based in London. His fiction has appeared in *Black Static*, *Nightscript*, *The Lonely Crowd*, *Unthology*, *Not One of Us*, *Humanagerie*, *Nox Pareidolia*, and Flame Tree's *Terrifying Ghosts* and *Beyond the Veil* anthologies, among others. His anthology *This Dreaming*

Isle was shortlisted for both a Shirley Jackson Award and a British Fantasy Award. His non-fiction has appeared everywhere from *Salon* to *The Guardian*, and a collection of his short fiction, *Only The Broken Remain*, was published by Black Shuck Books in November 2020. He is an editor at award-winning publisher Unsung Stories, and works freelance at momuseditorial.co.uk.

Website: http://dancoxon.com

Paul Currion is his own worst pseudonym. He has published fiction in *The White Review*, *Nature*, *Going Down Swinging* and various anthologies; non fiction in *Granta*, *The White Review*, *Aeon*, *The Guardian* and others; and installation work at the Vienna Biennale, Berlin Soundout!, and TransEuropa Belgrade.

Website: www.currion.net/

C.R. Dudley is a writer, artist and mind explorer. She is fascinatated by the human condition, in particular the effect future technology might have on our psyche, and sees everything she creates as part of one continuous artwork.

She started blogging in 2014 as a way to express the ideas stemming from her studies in Jungian psychology and mysticism. Her first few stories were distributed as hand-stitched art zines in aid of a mental health charity, and her style became known for its multi-layered narratives.

In 2017 she founded Orchid's Lantern, a small independent press for metaphysical fiction. She is the author of two short story collections, *Fragments of Perception* and *Mind in the Gap*, which have been described as 'unique philosophical fiction' and 'strange, uplifting and soul searching'.

C.R. Dudley lives in North Yorkshire and is a lover of forest walks, pizza, tequila and dark music.

Twitter: @c_r_dudley. Website: www.orchidslantern.com/

Pippa Goldschmidt is a writer based in Edinburgh and Frankfurt. She's the author of the novel *The Falling Sky* and the short story collection *The Need for Better Regulation of Outer Space*, as well as co-editor (with Tania Hershman) of *I Am Because You Are*, an anthology of short stories and essays inspired by general relativity.

Her work has been broadcast on BBC Radio 4 and published in a variety of places including *Mslexia, Litro, Gutter, Times Literary Supplement* and the *New York Times*, as well as anthologies such as *A Year of Scottish Poetry* (Macmillan) and *Best American Science and Nature Writing 2014* anthology (Houghton Mifflin).

Her most recent project was co-editing (with Drs Gill Haddow and Fadhila Mazanderani) *Uncanny Bodies*, an anthology of fiction and non-fiction inspired by Freud, cyborgs and the history of Edinburgh, and published by Luna Press in 2020.

Twitter: @goldipipschmidt. Website: www.pippagoldschmidt.co.uk

Frances Gow is a writer of speculative fiction which crosses the boundaries between Science Fiction, Fantasy and Horror with publication in a variety of magazines, including: *The New Accelerator, Electric Spec, MIR Online, STORGY Magazine and Cemetery Moon*. She collaborated with her father, DC Laval, on a series of medieval fantasy adventures for young adults, called *The Carentan Series*, published by Double Dragon Publishing.

Twitter: @FrancesGow. Website: www.francesgow.co.uk/

Paul A. Green's poetry includes *The Gestaltbunker* (Shearsman Books 2012), in which 'Brain Gun' first appeared and *Shadow Times* (QBS Publications 2019). His speculative fiction consists of *The Qliphoth* (LibrosLibertad 2007), *Beneath the Pleasure Zones I* and *II* (Mandrake 2014, 2016) and *Dream Clips of the Archons* (QBS Publications 2020) as well as the short story collection *An Advanced Guide to Radial City* (QBS Publications 2020). His plays for radio and stage are collected in *Babalon and Other Plays* (Scarlet Imprint 2015).

Website: www.paulgreenwriter.co.uk/

David Gullen is a writer and editor with work recently published by *F&SF* magazine, Eibonvale Press, and Newcon Press. His work has been short-listed for the James White Award, placed in the Aeon Award, and won the British Fantasy Society short story competition. He has been a judge for the Arthur C. Clarke and James White Awards, and is the current Chair of the Milford SF convention in the UK. David was born in Africa, baptised by King Neptune, and raised in England. He lives in South London with the fantasy writer Gaie Sebold behind several tree ferns.

Twitter: @dergullen. Website: http://www.davidgullen.com/

John Houlihan is a British science fiction and fantasy writer, journalist and game designer and is best known for his 'Seraph Chronicles' series comprising *The Trellborg Monstrosities*, *The Crystal Void* and *Tomb of the Aeons* and *Before the Flood*.

He has also written 'The D'Bois Escapades', featuring his latest novel *Feast of the Dead*, and has also published a novel, *Tom or The Peepers' and Voyeurs' Handbook* and *The Cricket Dictionary*. He was editor of *Dark Tales from the Secret War*, a 13 story anthology of weird World War 2 tales and was script writer for *The Forest of Fear* videogame.

Twitter: @Johnh259. Website: www.john-houlihan.net/

Mark Huntley-James has a PhD in Physics, worked in R&D and then financial software, as well as doing the usual mundane things like traditional English clog dance, amateur theatre stage crew, keeping bees, historical re-enactment, and writing science-fiction and fantasy. He lives on a small farm in Cornwall with his partner and a menagerie of cats, poultry and sheep.

Twitter: @MarkH_J.

Website: www.markhuntleyjames.wordpress.com

Simon Ings is a critic, journalist and writer who keeps circling back to science fiction between forays into science, history and the sorts of literary novels that garner more reviews than sales. He was the editor of the short-lived design-fiction magazine *Arc*, then *New Scientist* arts editor for six years, and now he works for himself, crouched in a freezing cold flat on a hill in London, writing for the *Financial Times*, *The Times*, *The Spectator* and *The Telegraph*. His latest non-fiction is *Stalin and the Scientists* (Faber, October 2016). *The Smoke*, his most recent novel, was published by Gollancz in February 2018. He has also edited big reprint anthology *We Robots* (Head of Zeus, 2020).

Website: www.simonings.net/

Viraj Joshi is a designer, technologist, and futurist. He produces curious objects and fiction with great affinity towards our technological and social futures.

He currently works at Fjord, Stockholm after Royal College of Art (MA), and Imperial College, London (MSc). His work explores human-computer interactions, speculative design and futures, and emerging technology, and has received several international accolades, including an exhibition at the Science Museum, London, and with the United Nations.

Instagram: @virajvjoshi. Website: virajvjoshi.com

How do we determine causation? This and other questions about disease plague **Jessica Laine**'s visceral brain. She recently joined Imperial College London as a postdoctoral researcher, after completing her PhD in Epidemiology and moving across the pond from the US. Her work usually graces the pages of scientific journals, but she is seeking to expand into fictional and poetic prose to express thoughts on humanity and philosophy.

Twitter: @Laine_J_E_

Ken MacLeod is the author of seventeen novels from *The Star Fraction* (1995) to *The Corporation Wars: Emergence* (Orbit, 2017), and many articles and short stories. His novels and stories have received three BSFA awards and three Prometheus Awards, and several have been short-listed for the Clarke and Hugo Awards. In 2009 he was Writer in Residence at the ESRC Genomics Policy and Research Forum at Edinburgh University, and was Guest Selector for the Science Fiction strand at the Edinburgh International Book Festival 2017. Ken's novella *Selkie Summer* has just been published by NewCon Press. He is currently working on a space opera trilogy.

Website: https://www.kenmacleod.blogspot.com

Tim Maughan is an author and journalist using both fiction and non-fiction to explore issues around cities, class, culture, technology, and the future. His work regularly appears on the *BBC*, *New Scientist*, and *Vice/Motherboard*. His debut novel *INFINITE DETAIL* was published by FSG in 2019, and selected by *The Guardian* as their Science Fiction and Fantasy book of the year. He also collaborates with artists and filmmakers, and has had work shown at the V&A, Columbia School of Architecture, the Vienna Biennale, and on Channel 4. He currently lives in Canada.

Website: www.timmaughanbooks.com

Anne McKinnon is founder of theboolean.io, analysing today to make the best of tomorrow's technologies. As a journalist, Anne reports on the state of deep tech. She travels the world, seeing the most cutting-edge breakthroughs in art, technology, and media, interviewing leading executives, bootstrapped startups, artists, and engineers to build an accurate picture of the immersive technology ecosystem, and where it may end up.

Anne works with clients on groundbreaking projects at the intersection of gaming x entertainment x metaverse x innovation. She is an editor and contributing author to Forbes writer Charlie Fink's book *Convergence* on 5G and AR. Her short stories have been featured at Virtual Futures in London. She's a guest writer with VRScout, works with music artist Miro Shot touring live virtual reality concerts and has hosted global conference sessions in gaming & esports, startups, music, and tech. By writing speculative fiction, Anne explores the potential and influence of emerging technologies on our lives.

Website: http://www.theboolean.io/

Jane Norris writes speculative design fiction about our relationship to the objects and materials around us. She has written several short stories and read them at Virtual Futures events including 'Re-Pairing' published in the *Virtual Futures: Near-Future Fictions vol. 01* anthology and has a piece 'Writing Round the Outside' published in the literary journal *Lune*. Jane has written a regular Dictionary of Craft column in the Crafts Council *CRAFTS* magazine and opinion pieces for the design magazine *Fiera*. Her piece 'A View from the Throne' was published in the 'Toilet' issue of *Dirty Furniture*. She recently completed post-doc research in Critical Writing at the Royal College of Art. She has an essay 'Touching Knowledge' in *Meet Us in The Now*, an RCA book. Before joining Richmond University, Jane led a BA Hons in 3D Design for ten years. She is an Associate Dean at Richmond University, the American University in London. She is currently writing a climate fiction novel about sentient materials.

Contact: drjanenorris@gmail.com. Twitter: @janeviatopia

Dan O'Hara is a literary historian and philosopher of technology. He has taught at the universities of Oxford, Stanford, Warwick, Cologne, and NCH London, and was one of the founders of Virtual Futures in the 1990s. His D.Phil. was a history of the idea of the machine in literature, art, and philosophy since the Enlightenment. He has published widely on British and American literature, critical theory, and the evolution of technology. He has served as a committee chair of the British HCI (Human-Computer Interaction) Conference, is an invited member of the UK's All-Party Parliamentary Group on Artificial Intelligence, and has given evidence to the House of Lords Select Committee on Artificial Intelligence. His work in philosophy of technology is featured regularly by the BBC, in the mainstream press such as *New Scientist* and the *Economist*, in academic publications such as the *Journal of the History of Ideas*, and in specialist journals such as *Computing* and *IT Pro*. His most recent books are *Extreme Metaphors: Interviews with J. G. Ballard* (2012/14), and *Virtual Futures: Near-Future Fictions* (2019).

Twitter: @skeuomorphology. Website: danohara.co.uk

Stephen Oram writes science fiction. He is a founding curator for near-future fiction at Virtual Futures, a writer for sci-fi prototypers SciFutures, and a member of the Clockhouse London Writers. He is published in several anthologies and has two published novels. His collections *Eating Robots* and *Biohacked & Begging* have been praised by publications as diverse as The Morning Star and The Financial Times.

Twitter: @OramStephen. Website: www.stephenoram.net/

Jule Owen is a writer of novels and short stories about the impact of today's technology and energy use on possible versions of our future. She lives in London but was raised in the north of England and is therefore used to balancing often contradictory world-views in her head. By day she works in technology and gets a lot of ideas from taking reality a bit too far.

Contact: info@juleowen.com. Website: www.juleowen.com/

Adrian Reynolds is primarily a script writer, with experience of film, tv, theatre, and comics. His award-winning sf short film White Lily is one of the genre pieces he's proud of. Check out the Escapades page at adrianinspires.com for a link to that plus some of his other work. He's developing stories for feature film, tv, animation and comics that are getting attention; and does script development work.

Based in Nottingham, Adrian is taller than a medical height chart goes to. This provides further evidence to feed his suspicion that he is not of this world.

Jennifer Rohn is a practicing scientist at University College London as well as a novelist, journalist, public speaker, science communicator and pundit. She coined the term 'lab lit' to describe realistic novels featuring scientists as central characters. She founded the popular website LabLit.com to help promote the use of science and scientist characters in mainstream fiction, and to illuminate the world of scientists and laboratory culture. Jenny's writing has appeared in many places, including The Guardian, The Telegraph, The Times, BBC News, Nature and The Scientist.

Website: jennyrohn.com

Geoff Ryman has won the Nebula Award, the Arthur C. Clarke Award twice, the British Science Fiction Association award three times and 11 other science fiction and fantasy awards. He was the commissioning editor of *When it Changed* (Comma Press): an anthology of commissioned collaborations between scientists and writers and produced the '100 African Writers of SFF' on the Strange Horizons website.

Website: www.ryman-novel.com/category/home/

Antoine Saint Honoré studied Literature at university. For many (pleasant) years he worked as a receptionist. Since 1998 he has been writing a book about Goa and the death drive. He is very influenced by Borges, Isabelle Eberhardt and Basho. He once had the support of a literary agent but failed (through extreme slowness) to supply precise/sample chapters when asked.

Contact: AntoineSt@hotmail.com

Britta Schulte writes. From one-line dystopias to PhD theses, they create technologies that we might get, to ask if we really want them. Stories are spread over the internet, self-published zines and selected anthologies.

Twitter: @brifrischu. Medium: @brifrischu

Sophie Sparham is a writer and spoken word artist from Derby. Her debut poetry collection *Please Mind the Gap* features a foreword from Benjamin Zephaniah. Sophie has written poetry commissions for Writing East Midlands, BBC Radio 4, The V&A and The People's History Museum. Sophie gave a Ted X Talk at the University of Kent about how spoken word can improve our cultural awareness.

Sophie co-hosts *Word Wise* with Jamie Thrasivoulou, which won Best Regular Spoken Word Night at the Saboteur Awards 2019. She was longlisted for the Out Spoken Page Prize 2019.

Twitter: @SophieSparham. Website: www.sophiesparham.co.uk

David Turnbull is a member of the Clockhouse London group of genre writers. He writes mainly short fiction and has had numerous short stories published in magazines and anthologies, as well as having stories read at live events such as Liars League London, Solstice Shorts and Near-Future Fictions. He was born in Scotland, but now lives in the Catford area of London.

Contact: davidm_turnbull@hotmail.com.

Website: www.tumsh.co.uk/

Tom Ward's most recent publication was *Virtual Futures: Near Future Fictions vol. 1*, edited with Dan O'Hara and Stephen Oram. He studied the ethics and consequences of emerging technologies under Dominic Pettman, Eugene Thacker and McKenzie Wark during his recent MA at The New School for Social Research in New York. His dissertation discussed the connexions between suicidal ideation and AI. Currently, he is working on a novel and a collection of short stories as well as studying law with the hope of finding ways to challenge irresponsible deployments and uses of technology.

Contact: thomaswardwork@gmail.com

Born in England to New Zealand parents, **Jamie Watt** is now settled in Dublin, Ireland after a nomadic youth in continental Europe. He has degrees in English & Italian and Film Studies from University College Dublin. Jamie has worked in film, television and music but is not yet irrevocably cynical. Another short story "Sequence" was published in *Virtual Futures: Near Future-Fictions Volume 1.*

He is currently working on Arcana, an anthology of fantasy novellas and developing a TV series with a BAFTA winning film-producer.

Contact: jamwatt@gmail.com

Bea Xu is a multi-disciplinary psychic worker who writes visionary fiction. She is interested in seizing the means of reality production and founded a community called LUNARCHY with Radical Anthropology Group in 2018. Bea studies transpersonal psychotherapy at CCPE and is working to mitigate climate catastrophe.

The first version of this story was submitted in December 2017 and at the writing of its second incarnation, new narratives were weaved to better reflect this author's present optimism about humanity's future. This might well be the first story of Bea's adult life in print but will hopefully remain the gloomiest of them all – which is a sentiment she feels blessed to express at this juncture.

Keep fighting the good fight; sooner or later we will win.

Instagram: @ _fei__fei. Soundcloud: beaxu.xyz

Also from NewCon Press

Burning Brightly edited by Ian Whates
Celebrating 50 years of Novacon, featuring a mix of original fiction and first time reprints of stories written by former Guests of Honour, including **Iain M. Banks, Peter F. Hamilton, Stephen Baxter, Justina Robson, Paul McAuley, Jaine Fenn, Adrian Tchaikovsky, Anne Nicholls, Geoff Ryman, Ian R. MacLeod, Juliet E. McKenna,** and more…

Saving Shadows – Eugen Bacon
Prose poetry and speculative micro-lit pieces by renowned author Eugen Bacon. Forty-eight pieces in all: twenty-six previously published and twenty-two written specially for this book. Complementing the written word are a series of full page illustrations commissioned by the author from artist Elena Betti; thirty-five stunning images that enhance the reading experience.

Shopocalypse – David Gullen
Josie and Novik embark on the ultimate roadtrip. In a near-future re-sculpted by climate change, they blaze a trail across the shopping malls of America in a printed intelligent car (stolen by accident), with a hundred and ninety million LSD-contaminated dollars in the trunk. Pursued by vengeful drug cartels and the agents of corrupt authority, they set out to bring down the system, buying shoes and cameras to change the world.

Wergen: The Alien Love War – Mercurio D. Rivera
A sophisticated alien race biochemically infatuated with humans, the Wergens crave us, while we need their technology. We exploit them, until they find a way around their addiction. From the towering skyscrapers of Earth to the methane lakes of Titan, from the ice-plains of Pluto to distant alien gas giants, these stories of unrequited love play out against the cosmic backdrop of conflict between the two species.